OKIES
Selected Stories

OKIES
Selected Stories

by
Gerald Haslam

➜

Peregrine Smith, Inc.
SANTA BARBARA AND SALT LAKE CITY

1975

First edition, 1973
Second edition, 1974
published by New West Publications

Third edition, 1975
published by Peregrine Smith, Inc.

The author wishes to thank the editors of *Arizona Quarterly*, *Journal 31*, and *Dakota Farmer* for permission to reprint stores which originally appeared in those journals.

Library of Congress Cataloging in Publication Data

Haslam, Gerald W
    Okies.

    CONTENTS: The doll.—California Christmas.—Smile.—Sally let her bangs hang down.—Campañeros.—Cowboys.—Passage.—Dishonor.—Wild goose: memories of a valley summer. [etc.]
    I. Title.
PZ4.H3495OK4   [PS3558.A724] 813'.5'4   75-26947
ISBN 0-87905-042-X

Manufactured in the United States of America

For Pat Brooks, Fred Dominguez, and Lionel Williams

Contents

The Doll

Mrs. Hollis saw them walking up her driveway toward the front porch, two ragged boys holding hands, the larger pulling the smaller. Okies, she thought, from the camp in Riverview; I wonder what they want, walking so boldly in a respectable neighborhood. Something really ought to be done about them. A person didn't know what to expect next. Just yesterday a skinny, one-legged man had knocked at her door and tried to sell her a can of salve; before that it had been another scrawny man trying to sell garden seeds. Lord, they were spreading into nice neighborhoods like vermin. They'd be wanting to move in next.

Before the boys reached her front steps Mrs. Hollis walked heavily into the doorway and talked through the screen: "Yes?" she said.

The day was oppresively hot, even in the shade of the porch, but the Okies stopped in full sunlight on the front lawn. The larger boy, lean with dirty-looking yellow hair that contrasted with his deeply sun-browned skin, answered in a flat nasal voice: "Lookin' fer work, lady. Kin we mow yer lawn er anythang?"

Although her lawn was indeed shaggy, she didn't want this drippy-nosed Okie near her any longer than necessary. "Well I haven't got anything for you boys to do, and I doubt if anyone in this neighborhood does," she replied curtly, feeling an immediate rush of satisfaction at having put them in their place. Turning, she reentered the relative coolness of her house.

"Lady," she heard the boy whine.

"What is it?" She returned to the doorway. They don't even know when they're not wanted, she thought; they're like animals.

"Could we have us a drank from yonder hose?" The boy's voice was inflectionless, almost exhausted; he pointed toward a rubber hose curled like a sunning serpent near a metal spigot.

Well that's typical, thought Mrs. Hollis, next thing you know they'll be asking for a meal. "Be quick about it. I've got my bridge club coming, you know!" She turned away from the door again, but abruptly changed her mind, deciding to watch them; they'll steal anything if a person isn't careful.

The yellow-haired boy ambled toward the hose, saying over his shoulder to the smaller boy, "Come own, Henery."

Mrs. Hollis glanced at the smaller boy, gazed away, then shot her eyes back at him in a huge, swallowing look. He wasn't a boy at all! He was a little man! His flat, pasty face was covered by a filigree of fine wrinkles, and he grinned vacantly at her, his teeth pointed like a shark's, his eyes like two tiny ball bearings set in uncooked dough. She felt something like a soft flower opening in her middle, warming her stomach, filling her with an imprecise sense of foreboding and fascination. The little lined face continued to grin at her, its features immobile. Mrs. Hollis fidgeted, shifting her weight from one thick leg to the other. "Uh, hello," she finally mumbled, her voice less harsh and certain than before.

The face, moon-like with metallic eyes, its contour broken by a thin nose as sharp and curved as an owl's beak, remained unchanged, sharp teeth grinning, reminding her vaguely of a wetting doll she'd owned as a little girl.

Before the spigot holding the hose, the yellow-haired boy knelt and slurped heavily the gushing water. He stood after a moment and called to the little man: "Come own, Henery. Take you a drank." Henry obeyed, shuffling with the undisciplined jerks of a string-tangled marionette.

"What's wrong with him?" Mrs. Hollis asked the boy.

"He's a idyet," the boy answered absently, "born in sin."

"Born in *what*?"

"In sin. His ma warn't mur'd."

My Lord, thought Mrs. Hollis, what's wrong with those people, letting a boy know about such things. Yet her fascination compelled her to look once more at the little man who was drinking now, then asked the boy: "Is he your brother?"

"No'm. He's m' uncle."

The idiot stood up and said to the boy, "Na nwa goo."

"Shore is," the boy replied.

"What did he say?" asked Mrs. Hollis.

"Said the water's good."

After turning the water off and grasping one of Henry's hands, the boy said to his uncle, "What do ya say?"

"Nan nyou," Mrs. Hollis heard the idiot mumble; she noticed how small his hands were as he wiped his glistening mouth, and how perfect, like an exquisite doll's. Her own plump hands were swollen and splotched with glandular middleage, and her attempts to fade them with creme had only bleached them so that she appeared to be wearing pink gloves, with splotches.

The boy feigned a departure, hesitated, then turned to Mrs. Hollis. "You ain't got some little thang we could do fer a samich do you lady. We're mighty hongry."

Still transfixed by the idiot's guileless grin, Mrs. Hollis vacillated. "We'll do most anythang," said the boy hopefully. Glancing at him, Mrs. Hollis noticed he too had an owl's beak nose and that his gray eyes were rimmed with red and streaked. His face was, save for its grainy tan, colorless and void. Well, she thought, I can't turn away the hungry, but I've got to hurry because my bridge club's coming. "You wait on the porch," she ordered with a hint of her previous curtness, "I'll bring you something."

As she walked back through the house past the card table laden with cookies and little liverwurst (she called it "paté") sandwiches without crusts, she heard the boy's whining voice talking to his uncle. She supposed the boy to be about twelve years old, large for his age though thin, with a viperene face too wide at the forehead, too narrow at the chin; his eyes were not aligned. He wore faded blue jeans that exposed bony ankles, and a torn tee-shirt that was on backwards so that it hugged his throat in front (Mrs. Hollis's own plump throat had grown a little uncomfortable looking at it) and drooped in back. His neck was dirty. The little man, whose hair was mousy gray, wore short bib overalls with no shirt. Neither wore shoes.

She brought each of them a peanut butter sandwich wrapped in wax paper. "You eat these after you've gone, hear," she told them, "I've got my bridge club today."

"You ain't told us what work to do, lady."

"Never mind that. Take your sandwiches. I'm expecting my bridge club any time."

"We can come back after if you want, lady," said the boy, making no effort to take the sandwiches.

"Oh, all right. You come back tomorrow and I'll have some job for you."

"Thank you, lady," he said, taking the food. "What do ya say, Henery?"

"Nan nyou."

Later, at the bridge table, Frances Bryant had brought it up. "There was an Okie came by my house," she reported between nibbles at a frosted cookie, nodding slowly and raising one eyebrow, "selling some kind of remedy. He was the awfulest thing I ever saw, all skinny and with one leg cut off."

"Well," replied Mrs. Tatum, the newest club member, knowledgeably.

"And," Frances continued, "have you ever noticed their skin, how it's so dark and blotchy. They've all got colored blood, you know."

"My Ev says they're part Gypsie, kid," interjected Mary Cannon.

Frances nodded. "Could be. Lord knows they act like Gypsies, what with never settling down or taking steady jobs. All the same, Gypsie or not, they're still part colored."

"They're certainly not much better than niggers," Hope Cuen added. "They're certainly not."

They sat with corpulent dignity around a small card table, their soft bodies scented against sweat with strong cologne, their plump little fingers poised away from their hands—like fat white worms tempting unwary fish—while the ladies nibbled cookies.

"Well, Winnie, You're certainly quiet today," observed Frances. "You and Claude have a fight?" The other ladies giggled.

"Oh, no," Mrs. Hollis hid her welling desire to put Frances in her place, "I've just got a lot on my mind."

"You're always day-dreaming Winnie," Frances said with a laugh, exchanging a knowing look with Mrs. Tatum. "You'd better be careful or you'll have those Okies moving in on you. You have to be alert in this world."

"Amen," added Hope Cuen. "Amen."

"Not much chance of that—them moving in, I mean," Mrs. Hollis sputtered impotently. She was always helpless before Frances and wasn't even sure she liked her; she could only think of things to say to Frances after their one-sided verbal exchanges were long over.

Frances continued, ignoring Mrs. Hollis: "Well you girls heard about what happened at the First Baptist Church, I guess." She looked about her, they hadn't heard. "Well, last week a whole family of Okies came to the services just as big as you please."

"Oh no, kid."

"What did the congregation do?" asked Mrs. Hollis.

"What could they do, being Christians and all? They left them alone, of course. But right after services Reverend Willis and some men went over to them and, nice as you please, told them they weren't wanted."

"Of course."

"That was a nice way to handle things."

"Well, that's just what I thought when I heard," hissed Frances, "but listen to this: that Okie man got mad and started a fight!"

"Oh no."

"The Sheriff had to come and break it up and take him to jail."

"It's too good for them," Mrs. Tatum observed with finality.

"That's just what I think," Frances said. "Now listen to *this*"—she paused as though to savour their attention—"you know that crazy Durant woman, the one who drinks and whose daughter is so loose, well she got angry at Reverend Willis and caused a scene right in front of everybody."

"What in the world did she do, kid?" drooled Mary Cannon.

"Well, I don't know. *Everything.* Screamed. Shouted. Quoted the Bible incorrectly as usual. She even claimed Jesus said everyone was supposed to love their neighbors, so that means everyone's supposed to love Okies! You know how crazy she is."

"What a shame," said Mrs. Hollis.

"They certainly aren't my neighbors," Mrs. Tatum gasped, "not those Okies."

"We'll I'll tell you one thing"—Frances nodded with certainty—"Jesus didn't mean *them*." She glared triumphantly at the other women for a moment. "He didn't mean them," she said once more.

Later, just as the ladies were readying to leave, Mrs. Hollis thought to ask Frances about her brother who hadn't been right. What had ever happened to him?

Frances looked nervous. "Why in the world do you ask?"

"Oh, I just got to thinking that the last time I saw him was when you had bridge club two years ago and your parents were visiting. Remember? And they'd brought your brother with them. He was such a quiet little man."

"Well, when Mother and Father died so close to one another, Brother didn't have anywhere to stay, so Charles and I arranged for him to live up north." She hurried with her final cookie, but Mrs. Hollis wasn't letting go so easily.

"Where up north, dear?"

"Well, at Sonoma. It's lovely there, not hot," she added glancing round the table.

"At the *state* hospital?" Mary Cannon asked. "Oh, kid."

"Well. Well, he's happier with his own kind."

Mrs. Hollis almost inquired if his sister wasn't his own kind, but she wasn't certain Frances would take too kindly to that in her present agitated state, so she let it pass and the afternoon ended for her on an unusual note of triumph.

Mrs. Hollis hummed in her too-warm kitchen; only if she could convince Claude to accept a salad for dinner in the summer, only if she could. Still, no mere physical heat could disturb the deep pleasure that softened and sweetened her: Frances put in her place for once. And almost an accident at that, for she hadn't dreamed Frances had done—or even *could* do—such a thing. Imagine, her own brother sent to a lunatic asylum. Her own brother. And all Mrs. Hollis had intended was to ask about the little man; those Okies had reminded her of him.

Dinner was unusually gay and afterwards she and Claude walked slowly through the Oildale heat to the ice cream shop on Woodrow Street and each slurped a double cone. Then she sat on the front porch as usual while he watered the front lawn in thick, dimming twilight, Claude shouting pleasantries across the street into other yards where people whose houses they'd never entered shot sleek, silvery sprays over yellow grass. A clatter of children swept up and down the block on or after a roller-skate scooter. When Claude finished, they went into the house and Mrs. Hollis impulsively suggested a game of Monopoly. It was an unusually happy evening for them, and later, in spite of the heat, they made it even happier.

Mrs. Hollis always slept late—Claude had for years arisen early and taken breakfast at a diner—so she hadn't finished her morning coffee when the door bell rang. Stealing a clandestine glance at the front porch through a barely-drawn side curtain, she was stunned to see a flat, grey eye pressed against the glass opposite her's, staring back; it was the idiot. Mrs. Hollis smiled her embarrassment, then joggled to the door and opened it, keeping the screen locked.

"Mornin' lady," said the straw-haired boy.

"Oh. Why, good morning."

They stood facing one another through the fine mesh for several moments, then the boy spoke again. "We come about that job of work."

"Oh. Why, yes. Just let me finish my coffee and I'll tell you what to do." Out of the corner of her eye she noticed that the little man still stared into the side window.

"Awright lady."

She turned back toward the kitchen only to hear: "Lady?"

"Yes."

"You ain't got no extra coffee do you. Me and Henery ain't had us no breakfast to eat." The boy's voice was flat, with no hint of either demand or plea or even expectation. An automatic "No!" flashed into Mrs. Hollis, and she turned quickly, her jaws tightening; she ought to put that boy in his place. She hesitated, looking from the boy to the man who still stood next to the window, then back to the boy again. "Well, I'll get you something. You can pick up the dog dirt from the lawn—there's a shovel in the garage—and then start mowing. Make sure you rake up the clippings; I don't want them turning brown on the grass. The lawn mower's in the garage too."

Mrs. Hollis put a fresh pot of coffee on to perk and made sandwiches, something they could eat outside. And she watched them working on the lawn through the window over the kitchen sink. The large thin boy pushed the lawn mower, the delicate little man raking industriously, if sloppily, behind him. The boy stopped every now and then and said something to the man, who nodded vigorously, then went on raking.

Why they really weren't half bad she mused, not when you knew how to handle them. They worked. And there was that idiot man living right with them, she guessed, right with his own family, working, being taken care of, really happy. Wait until Frances and the bridge-club hear about this! It's a shame, though, them coming to California where they're not wanted. They should have stayed in Oklahoma or wherever it was they really belonged. But still, they weren't half bad if you knew how to treat them.

The boy wolfed down the sandwich in an instant and drank the hot, unblown coffee with grimacing gulps. The man ate slowly, nibbling and chewing with rapid grins for a long time before swallowing, his tiny hands squeezing the bread a bit too tight so that catsup and mayonnaise dripped—a pink blot—unnoticed by him onto his overall bib. The boy followed Mrs. Hollis's eyes to the gooey stain and told his uncle to wipe himself, handing him a kerchief that was clearly a ragged square torn from an old sheet.

The boy drank a second cup of coffee, then they returned to work, mowing and raking steadily over the nearly half-acre of lawn, resting occasionally in the hot morning and drinking from Mrs. Hollis's garden hose. She watched them from the cool cavern of her house, sitting in front of the blower much of the time. They're hard working people, she thought, and not half bad. At least they take care of their own, not like some I know.

By the time they finished the lawn and trimmed the edges it was nearly lunch, so she brought them sandwiches and lemonade. She tried to prompt the boy into telling her about his family; much to her dissatisfaction, he said little, answering her with apparent candor but no enthusiasm. She began to feel there was something *basic* about these people, though she didn't know exactly what. The doll-like little man grinned and ate, ate and grinned. A slightly triumphant, exhilarated mood crept into Mrs. Hollis as she watched them eat. She had tamed them; she had them doing her bidding and acting properly. Mrs. Hollis gave each of them one of her good chocolate-covered cherries after lunch, the ones wrapped in red foil.

She set them to digging up dandelions and crab grass in the afternoon, telling them it was perfectly all right if they did the patches in shade under trees first in the glaring heat, then she retired to the couch under the blower for her afternoon nap.

She had just fallen asleep—surely she hadn't slept long—when a persistent tapping at the front door roused her roughly from the freedom of empty slumber, she drowsed awake but unaware for several moments before her mind focused on the sound. Arising heavily, Mrs. Hollis's legs felt thick, and her dress pressed to her with perspiration; her face remained creased where the pillow had been creased.

It was the boy. "What do you want?" she groggily asked.

"Kin we use yer bathroom, lady? We gotta piss."

His final word hit her with a dull jolt of revulsion. "You *what?*"

"We gotta piss," he repeated.

The word even sounded filthy. Mrs. Hollis felt her neck and face swelling with anger. "There are limits, young man," she sputtered, "there are limits. You can not use my bathroom. You can finish your work and leave!" She slammed the door, her stomach churning, near tears, and hurried into the kitchen to fix a cup of coffee. "Piss" echoed within her, and deep inside her mouth, just where her throat started, she felt the warm discomfort that preceded vomiting, but she caught herself, grasping the sink with both hands until nausea passed; she was finally fully awakened. That nasty word. She went into her bathroom, her pride, with its pink rug and curtains, and washed her puffed face, brushed her hair, then bathed herself lightly with cooling toilet water.

Back in the kitchen her coffee was ready. She looked out the window and saw the Okies under her pepper tree talking. They're not children she reassured herself, they can hold it. I did the right thing. You don't just invite people you don't know to use your bathroom; after all, there are limits. Besides, there was that nasty word. They can hold it.

In spite of herself, Mrs. Hollis mellowed as she sipped her coffee and watched them work. They do have to go just like anyone else, she thought, but where? Not in her bathroom surely. And not outside where the neighbors could see something so nasty. No solution came to her, so she again decided they could hold it until they got home, or at least to the Golden Bear gas station up on Chester Avenue. She hated that word, but was a little sorry she'd told them to finish work and leave. Okies probably couldn't help it, talking like that. Why her own brother-in-law sometimes slipped and said it. With all the little jobs around the house that wanted doing, she decided to forgive them and tell them to come back tomorrow to fix the roof.

After taking a dollar from her purse, she walked onto the porch and called them from their tasks; they could finish weeding tomorrow in the morning when it wasn't so hot. They walked to the porch, the little man bent forward a bit as though he'd stiffened-up while weeding, and for an instant she wondered how old he really was. The Okies stood below her on the walk side-by-side.

"You can quit for today. Here's a dollar for your work" —the boy quickly snatched it—"and I'll want you back tomorrow morning to finish the weeds and do another little job I have for you." She heard the boy cackle with a high, hollow sound. "What's so funny young man?"

The boy who had been looking at his uncle, turned smirking toward her and said: "Looky. He pissed hisself."

A growing wetness darked the little man's faded overalls, spreading shapelessly on his lap and his legs, urine running in thin yellow rivulets down his dusty ankles and feet, cutting faintly muddy paths, and puddling on Mrs. Hollis' cement walkway. His little doll face grinned stiffly.

A wave of nausea instantly overcame Mrs. Hollis; she slammed through the front door and lurched toward the bathroom, vomiting first in the hall, then in the bathroom on her pink rug. Again and again her body purged itself while she, like a suffering spectator, knelt before the toilet and her uncluttered brain vomited too, drawing deep from a reservoir within her. "Jesus didn't mean them," raced through her mind. "He didn't. He wouldn't. He didn't."

California Christmas

Things was powerful hard that first winter after we come to California. Daddy, and other farmers too, I reckon, just figured the sun shone all the year round out west and jobs went a-begging, but that ain't how it was. We was camped with some other folks right alongside the Kern River near Bakersfield. Daddy he'd found him a little work in the crops around there, and he had signed for a job with some oil companies; he was waiting to be hired and just hanging on with what he could pick up at day labor. Them oil fields looked mighty good to men with families to support; they looked like hope. Daddy figured he could make as much wages just working around Bakersfield as he could trying to follow crops all over the state; anyways Momma was sick and our truck was about give out. So we stayed in Riverview. Besides, there was always that chance he could get on with an oil company; he just pined for that.

It rained some that winter and the river climbed up the levee and scared hell out of us; we didn't have much left, but we sure didn't want to lose it. But praise Jesus the levee held. Mostly it was just cold and terrible foggy, a grainy grey fog that even made breathing hard. None of us never seen nothing like it back home on the farm, and it got lots of folks to talking about how much they missed Oklahoma. Us kids didn't have good clothes or even shoes, so we couldn't go to school. Momma said she surely prayed Daddy could get steady work so us kids could go to school, but she wasn't going to send us looking like scarecrows because she knew what would happen. It just seemed like folks wasn't too friendly toward us in California.

Daddy had fixed up a cabin for us out of whatever wood he found and cardboard. We lived in it, bundled up in all the clothes we did own and still cold. It must have been comical to see us looking like pale-faced Eskimos, but we didn't laugh none then, I'll tell you. Old sunny California just froze us half to death.

I don't believe none of us kids would have remembered Christmas that year, except one day the sun broke through so a bunch of us walked all the way to Oildale and saw a giant Christmas tree in front of the grade school there. That done it. We hustled ourselves home and commenced worrying poor Momma, us not realizing she was poorly. Momma she looked mighty sad, like she was gonna bawl, and she told us not to think too much about it. Well, before long we taken every kid from the camp to see that big old tree with its electric lights and fake snow. That tree looked ready to sprout presents any time.

Come the day before Christmas, Daddy couldn't find no work. He just fussed around the cabin, patching here and there and working on the stove. After while he went outside and squatted with other men talking about hard times. Well, all of a sudden up drives these two big shiny cars and out steps a preacher and some ladies. The preacher he opened the back of his car and commenced unloading big baskets filled with food and one filled with presents.

What's this? Daddy asked them. This is our annual Christmas basket program for the needy, said the preacher. What church? Daddy asked him. The preacher he looked kind of confused and I figured he'd ask what difference it made. Baptist, the preacher finally answered. Daddy looked around at the other men; Just what I figured, he said. I knew I seen this preacher before. Member when we tried to worship at your church last summer and you run us off? Now that preacher he surely didn't want to remember.

One big old fat lady stepped up in front of the preacher real uppity like. Here we are trying to help you people, she kind of hollered, and this is the thanks we receive. Daddy he said real quiet: Why don't you folks help us by letting us worship Jesus with you then? Now wait a minute, the preacher sputtered, but a man from camp he said: We'd rather a decent church for our kids than all that food. You've got this all wrong, the preacher said, and that fat lady fumed at us. Daddy cut them both off: You folks think you're too good to pray with us. Well then we ain't good enough to take your handouts either. Get the hell out of here! All of a sudden Daddy sounded dangerous. I guess being hungry, and seeing folks sneer at his kids, and knowing his wife was sick, and not finding work, I guess it all just welled up.

The fat lady had been pouting and glaring, but when she looked at Daddy's face, she waddled back to her car without saying nothing. I thought Daddy might sock her. One little guy from our camp he said to the preacher: You better get out of here, mister. Them townfolks climbed all over each other getting back into their cars and the preacher reloaded his baskets in a big hurry and got back into his car. As they pulled away, the fat lady put her big old face out a

window and said she was going to sic the sheriff on us.
Daddy he spit a great big goober on her car and didn't miss
her face by much.

Them rich people was so busy scrambling away that
they plum forgot their basket of presents, and all us kids
gathered round and, without touching nothing, stayed
mighty close to it. Daddy looked like he'd kick that basket
clean into the river, but another man came over and he said
maybe Jesus hadn't forgot us after all. He said we shouldn't
be sitting around feeling sorry for ourselves, that we ought
to hold a worship service right there on the river bank next
morning. Daddy he agreed with the man and said it was true,
the baby Jesus was born in a pretty humble place hisownself.

Everything changed that quick. An old man said his
boys and him had caught them a mess of carp and the
women folk could cook them up for Christmas dinner. Another man said his family had some extra beans and Daddy
said we had coffee to share. Other folks said they could fry
some pan bread and boil some syrup. Everyone was grinning and looking excited, then Daddy said: If that shurf
don't show up, I reckon we just might find something to do
with these presents too. He winked at us kids, and the men
all laughed.

That evening we built a huge bonfire and everyone
gathered round it in thick fog to sing hymns and Christmas
carols with the Kern River a-sucking and a-gurgling in the
background. About the time Momma was fixing to put us
kids to bed, up pulled a car. We couldn't make it out clear
through the fog, but one man said: I believe it's the shurf.
Daddy he tensed up and I seen him reach into the pocket
where he kept his knife, then I heard Momma whisper his
name—Roy—and she touched his arm. The car's door
slammed and a deputy come out of the fog and kind of stood
on his heels a-looking at us. It seemed like nobody was
breathing.

Evening, the deputy finally said, everything all right?
Daddy said things was fine. The deputy, he said that a big
fire was sure welcome on a cold night and folks agreed;
Sholy, one skinny lady said real loud, it sholy is. I heard you
folks singing, the deputy told us, so I just thought I'd stop

in for a minute. You're welcome, the same lady said. The deputy reached for a pocket and I could feel Daddy kind of stiffen, then the deputy said he had him a couple of kids at home and would it be okey if he give each of us a piece of hard candy. We couldn't hardly believe it; we hadn't had much candy since we left the farm. Daddy hesitated, but Momma said much obliged, so Daddy kept quiet and the deputy give each of us a piece all wrapped in paper. Merry Christmas folks, the deputy said and off he went.

After the car pulled away, Daddy he shook his head. Damn, he said, it's like folks out here just change the rules come Christmas. And I'm thankful they do, Momma said. A man said it's Jesus makes em change. Jesus he's a workin man hisownself. He don't forget workin folks. Amen, a lady added. Besides, another man said, these ain't bad folks out here. They're just skeered, skeered as they can be. They figure we might get their jobs, see. A lady said maybe we ought to pray for them, so we did.

Christmas morning every kid in camp had a gift. My sister Vondalee she got gloves and my big brothers, Earl and Larance, both got little metal cars; me, I got a small square box and inside was a whistle. It was the best present I ever got, and I still got it hanging on my key chain.

That morning we had us a real back home worship service for baby Jesus and we all said a special thanks for being so blessed. We ate carp and beans, and drank coffee. Then we had us some pan bread with syrup for dessert. Lord, was I stuffed. Everyone gathered round the fire after we ate and told stories about home and other Christmases. It seemed like all the folks were smiling at each other, and pretty soon Momma and Daddy stood right there with their arms around each other, us kids giggling and pointing. California didn't seem half bad.

Smile

Art rolled hazily on his bed, snug beneath his covers, and peaked through the blurred lashes of half-opened eyes. Grey morning. It was fun to sneak a look at the room, fun and secret; no one could tell. Slowly, without moving his head, he panned the blotched wall, the tiny television, the hotplate, the table, the smile. Perched on the edge of the table, they grinned at him with submerged exaggeration. He opened his eyes fully, caught. Mornin', he said. Mornin', answered his teeth from the glass where they soaked.

The old man crawled upright in his bed and swung his bare feet onto the cold linoleum floor. Reaching under the bed, he withdrew a coffee can into which he urinated, then returned it to its place. I'll empty 'er later, he said to his dentures. After pulling on a ragged pair of socks, he scratched at a vague itch under one arm. Well, he observed, might as well make me some coffee. The smile agreed. Art stood, longjohns hanging from his spare frame, and started to heat water on the hotplate. Water warming, he shuffled to the top bureau drawer and withdrew a paper sack of day-old (three-days-old now) doughnuts and removed one. He returned to the hotplate and brewed a cup of instant with luke-warm water, then carried his breakfast to the small table.

Well, let's turn 'er on, he mumbled to the smiling teeth, flicking the television's switch as he spoke. He began dunking his hardened doughnut into bitter coffee, slurping on it. Graveyard stew, he cackled and the teeth laughed with him; it was an old joke between them. He gazed out the

room's lone window while he waited for the reluctant T.V. to blink and swerve into glowing life, seeing grainy fog that obscured the street only two floors below. Hell of a day, he muttered. Back in Galveston they never had no days like this.

On the screen a plump man bartered excitedly with what appeared to be a midget moose. In a moment the man was assaulted by a hail of ping-pong balls, and Art had to laugh, sneaking a glance at the smile to make sure it was enjoying the show too. Jeeze, Art said. A moment later a large teddy bear shuffled onto the screen and began a soft shoe dance. That's really a guy in a bear suit, Art explained.

He always turned the television's volume a little louder than necessary. He was the only tenant on his floor who owned a set; all the others sat in the lobby and watched the hotel's T.V. Art let the grubby bastards who lived around him know he owned his own set. I don't need them, by God; I don't need nobody.

Now a Negro man was reading a story on the screen, and Art turned to the smile: Niggers everywhere nowadays. It's all part of the International Communist Conspiracy, he explained. A damn shame them lettin' niggers take over the country. Back when I's a kid, me and Bucky Humphrey whupped us some uppity niggers. All niggers want is a good lickin'. Nowadays they got black guys workin, the same docks me and Bucky used to work. Jeeze.

Well, hell. Art leaned back and lit-up what was left of yesterday's cigar. On the set, a little rabbit had tricked the captain out of a bunch of carrots. Art chuckled, and the teeth smiled in shared joy when he glanced at them.

A dull thump on the wall alerted Art to a neighbor's displeasure. That damned O'Hara, he said, the crazy old wino. Just jealous because I got a T.V. of my own. This hotel is loaded with crumbs, Art told the smile. Blow it out of your ass, O'Hara. He turned the television up slightly.

All he needed was that damn O'Hara bothering him. He hadn't been feeling too hot lately, and no bum like O'Hara was gonna get to him. No siree. Besides, sick or well, he was a hell of a lot better shape than most of the walking stiffs in this hotel. Terrible looking bastards, all of 'em. One foot in the grave and the other on a banana peel.

A mushy commercial flashed onto the screen, the one that always reminded him of his daughter, and he felt something secret within himself swell and flow. He averted his face from the smile, hating the whole thing; just when he thought he'd forgotten her, some damn silly commercial brought her gushing dangerously into his guts. His only kid, yet she never wrote, never even sent him a card. No use blubbering, he told himself, she's like her momma was: a cold woman. From below the bed he pulled a nearly empty bottle of muscatel; wine closed the cold scar of loneliness that had suddenly opened, and got him feeling like a man again.

O'Hara thumped the wall once more, breaking Art's reverie. The son-of-a-bitch! Art increased the T.V.'s volume; that'll teach him, he said. What a place this is, a damn looney bin, full of crazy people. A bunch of lousy winos. A man can't have no peace.

An old movie had come on the set, John Wayne kicking hell out of Nips. Them was the days, by God. No long-haired commies screwed around with John Wayne. He knew what

to do with hippies and Nips and all them other gooks too.
Hell, there's even a Nip right in this hotel: Mr. Takeuchi.
Soooo nice, everyone likes him. That's the way Nips are,
tricky. Claims he had a kid killed in the war. Ought to ask
him which side his kid was on.

Art was on his feet again, gazing out the window.
Nothing to do, it cold out and all; no place to go. Not the
Senior Center: a bunch of bossy old bitches trying to tell
everyone what to do. Bingo. Square dancing. Not going
there no more. And that damn O'Hara punching on the wall.
Wait till there's a good machine gun fight on the set, by
God; O'Hara's gonna think I'm shooting at his scrawny ass.
That'll shut the old sot up. Art nudged the volume up
another touch.

Wish I had me another little bottle to get me through
this stinking day, though. No money, no nothin'; just barely
enough to eat on.

He sat down, looked at the set, then at the wall, then
stood, scratched himself and again stared into the grey,
sullen morning. Hell, he said, turning just as an ax thudded
within him. Oh! The ax struck and hacked at his chest from
within, emptying his stomach, searing his breath, stealing it,
tingling electric icicles into his limbs. Oh Christ, Christ on
a crutch!

From the floor where he wallowed in pain, struggling
stiffly like an inverted insect, Art tried to cry for help, but

could only groan: O'Hara! then croak: O'Hara! John Wayne decimated the Empire of Japan with loud slashing explosions, and Art knew his own sounds were futile.

His breath gone, retching pain filling him, Art could no longer struggle; his limbs froze in tense inactivity and colors began bursting in his head. His frantic eyes searched for one last glimpse, one last hope, but sensed only the teeth resting on the table, not smiling, but leering a death's head grin from the swollen exaggeration of the water glass.

Sally Let Her Bangs Hang Down

Me and Laverne Horn we taken our savings out from the bank and had these fancy shirts made up, the kind with different-colored sequins all over em. We had the lady put big green cactuses on the fronts with blue and red kinda stars around, and our names on the backs. And that ain't all. We went and bought us new Levis, and bright red bandanas. Only thing is we didn't have enough money left for boots, so we just polished up our loafers the best we could. And, praise Jesus, we looked pretty damned slick if I do say so myself.

See, me and Laverne we entered this talent contest at the Kern Theatre. They was givin the winner a tryout with a real Hollywood talent scout, plus twenty bucks, and me and Laverne we wanted to win pretty bad. We was roustabouts then at the Golden Bear tank farm out by Oildale, and we'd been playin our guitars and singin for the boys at work, and they said we was real good. We was, too. We knew all the old Bob Wills' songs, and Lefty Frizzell's, Maddox Brothers and Rose's, Hank Williams's, Ernest Tubb's, Hank Snow's, Jimmie Rodgers's, all of em; we knew their songs.

We knew we wasn't goin nowhere in the oil business too, us not even finishing junior high school, and we sure as hell didn't want to end up like the old guys out to the tank farm, all stove up, choppin weeds when we's fifty- or sixty-year-old, livin on bacon gravy. No sir.

That night me and Laverne we dressed up and slicked our hair down and went to the Kern Theatre to win. But we had to sit clean through a Buster Crabbe movie before this pimply usher come and got us and took us behind the stage. I'll tell you, my belly was just tight like it is when I'm fixin to fight. Goddamnit! We *needed* to win.

There was this here old guy that whistled like birds, and this here young guy—a fairy I think—that wore patent leather shoes and tap danced, grinnin all the time. After him come a fat gal who played the Hi-wine steel guitar and sweated. After her a real pretty gal come on and she sang one of them Eye-talian opera songs that nobody can understand so it must be good; she had great big tits.

Well, me and Laverne we went on last. We sang "Sally Let Your Bangs Down," me lead and Laverne harmony, and we done a hell of a job too. When we come to that part of the song:

> I seen Sally changin clothes,
> She was in a perfect pose,
> *Sally let your bangs ha-ang down!*

folks just liked to raise the roof, a-whoopin and a-hollerin. They was really took with us.

When everybody's done, the audience got to clap for each act, it was about even between the gal with the big tits and us. This fat guy that was a Hollywood talent scout, he was the announcer. He kindly bounced around the stage, touchin that pretty gal ever chance he got and gabbin away in the microphone. Well, he had the folks clap just for the gal and us, and it come out even again. He done it about three more times, him brushin up on that gal as much as he could, her givin him the come on. He looked like he's gettin hot to me.

Finally the fat guy he hollered: "Well, it was close ladies and gentlemen, but I believe the little lady is your choice." Lots of folks cheered, but some others booed.

"Well I'll be go to hell," Laverne grunted to me.

Me, I turned to Laverne and told him: "I'll whup that fat bastard directly!"

"He just wants to get him a piece of tail, I believe," Laverne said to me.

"I'll tell the son-of-a-bitch off," I said, and I meant it too. We'd come to win, and the son-of-a-bitch robbed us.

Meanwhile, old fat ass he's prancing around the stage

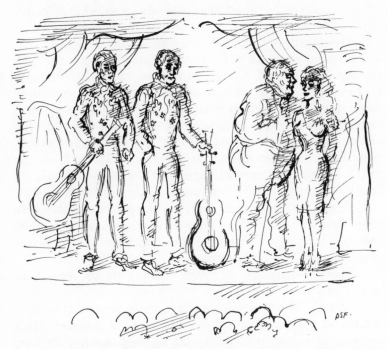

doin his best to feel up the winner right there. He shooed
all the others off stage, then he comes up to me and Laverne
and announced we's second place, as if everybody in the
picture show didn't know it. He commenced shakin Laverne's hand, then mine; his hand felt like fish guts. I pulled
him up close and hissed in his ear: "Eat shit!" while he's
shakin my hand.

"You're quite welcome," he said, pushin me and Laverne offstage, me gettin sorer all the time. Hell, he even
knocked some sequins off my shirt shovin me offstage, so
Laverne commenced gigglin like a damn fool. "What the
hell's wrong with you" I snapped at him, and he told me
my shirt it said "Tessie" on the back now instead of "Jessie." Damn but I was sore. "That ain't funny, Laverne!"

We had to leave backstage while the announcer carried
on about the pretty gal, and how Hollywood was callin, and
shit like that. He was one hell of a windbag, that guy.
Laverne he said let's go get us a beer, but I said no, I was
a-gonna wait in the lobby for old fat ass and really tell him

off. So Laverne he went over and set on this fancy couch by the popcorn machine while I stood by the door.

Directly here come ol fatso, making like a big shot with a cee-gar stuck in his puss, and he's just a huggin the little gal and carryin on. With em is this weasley guy, the manager of the picture show, and he looked to me like he figured he's a-gonna get some tail too, his face all red and wet. I started to go right up to em, then I heard this voice call my name real loud, so I turned and saw Weldon Magee, this ol boy that's a gauger out to the tank farm. Damnit, by the time I turned back around, fatso and everyone disappeared into the manager's office, so then I's sore at Weldon.

But ol Weldon sure made me forget in a hurry. He come over and said: "You boys done real good. Real good. I have to say you surprised me. You was a hell of a lot better than that gal, but just her bad luck she was purty."

Laverne he kinda squinted. "What do ya mean *bad* luck?" he asked.

"Hell," Weldon told us, "everyone knows this here contest is phony. That fat bastard is a local yokel. He's a-gonna give that gal twenty bucks, bed down with her, maybe even take some dirty pictures of her, then charge her the twenty dollars back to be her agent. Closest to Hollywood she'll get with him is a Hollywood bed."

"Well, I'll be got to hell!" I said, "How you know all that?"

"That's what I come over to tell you. You know the Wagon Wheel Inn out on Porterville Highway? Well my brother-in-law, Arvell, manages it, and he told me about old fat ass. And he asked me to come by here ever week to keep an eye out for local talent that could sing country songs. I believe he'd give you two a weekend job, good as you sang tonight."

"Good deal!" Laverne barked. "Good deal!"

I couldn't answer. We hardly knew Weldon, so him having kin runnin the Wagon Wheel never occurred to us. In fact I about half-figured Weldon was bullshittin, but he took us out to the Wagon Wheel that very evenin and introduced us to his brother-in-law. And by God ol Arvell was a good guy; he told us to practice up and come back on

Friday and he'd give us a try. Then he give us a glass of draft on the house.

Well, we had two days to practice, and we got hot after it. Here was our chance to break out of them oilfields, and we wasn't gonna blow it. We figured to learn some newer songs, so we tried "There Stands the Glass" the way Webb Pierce sang it but, Jesus, I like to lost a nut tryin to hit the high notes. Laverne he broke out laughin when he heard me try them high notes. "Damn," he said, "you better put one foot up on a high box next time you do that song, or you'll suck somethin right up into your belly," then he liked to fell over gigglin.

"Oh, to hell with you!" I told him, but I could see how comical it was.

Laverne he just couldn't quit laughin. "You reckon ol Webb has to wear a truss?" he asked, tears runnin down his face, and I couldn't hold out no longer and busted out laughin myownself. "Give that number a couple more tries," he told me, "and you gonna be singin them Eye-talian opera songs." Damn that Laverne was a funny guy.

Come Friday night and we's both pretty worried we'd mess-up some way and wreck things, even after all our practice. I liked to puked while we's waitin to go on stage, and ol Weldon he didn't help none, sneakin up with a silly grin on his face and askin "You ain't ascared are you?" "Hell no!" I told him, the simple bastard; how would he feel?

But we done real good, and Arvell he hired us on the spot.

Let me tell you that changed things considerable. It was like me and Laverne could see a future in what we was doin, and it even made diggin ditches and swampin barrels out to the tank farm a little easier, us knowin we'd be away from it one day. Better still, folks all of a sudden knowed us. Fellers at work that had ignored us started talkin, and folks on the streets even stopped us to say they enjoyed our singin. And the gals! Boy, howdy! We just took our pick of the cute girls, and older women too, that hung out at the Wagon Wheel. It was like horny-toad heaven, I'll tell you. If there was any singles come out to the Wagon Wheel that didn't like it, me and Laverne never met em. We diddled

ourselves cross-eyed on them beautiful things, and even
snapped naked pictures of some. I'd never even dreamed of
nothin so good.

In fact, Me and Laverne done so good at the Wagon
Wheel that after about two months Arvell he hired us to
sing ever night. And, you know, Jesus He was in on the
plan. The very day after we got the full-time job singin, we
drove out to the Wagon Wheel early while the after-work
crowd was still sippin suds before goin home. Well, me and
Laverne just set there nursin a draft when this ol boy in a
hardhat and oil-stained overalls come in the door and
marched right up to the bar. He kindly looked ever one over,
then he announced real loud: "Twelve year own the job,
boys, and I just got fard! Dranks're own me!"

He looked flat pitiful standing there about to spend his
severance pay on other guys' beer; he looked exactly like
what me and Laverne just escaped. So me, I went over to
him and told him Golden Bear was a-needin a couple boys.
He perked right up. "Hell, yeah," he said. "I'll go down
there first thang tomorra, by God. That's a good deal!"

Then he commenced tellin me what a good guy I was,
me bein a big star and all, and him wantin to buy me a beer.
He told me about his boy, and his wife that hated him, and
his ol momma that drove out here from Oklahoma near 40-
year-ago after his daddy got killed by a twister. Boy, howdy,
could that guy talk. Still, you can see how Jesus made the
plan, because when me and Laverne went out to visit our
pals at Golden Bear, there was that same ol boy on the business end of a hoe.

And that ain't all. It wasn't but a couple months after
we went full time at the Wagon Wheel that me and Laverne
got a chance on the Kousin Ken T.V. show in Bakersfield,
and ol Kousin Ken he hired us reg'lar. I went out and
bought me a big, shiny Harley-Davidson soon as I got my
first paycheck. We's eatin beefsteak stead of beans by then,
wearin tailor-mades stead of hand-me-downs. Yessir, we
had us plenty fancy duds, sequin shirts and jackets too.
And we had this here Fillipino barber that cut our hair to
look like Porter Wagoner's and even used hair spray.

By that time I's writing some of the songs we sung,

and ol Kousin Ken he said he'd try to get us a record contract. We hired this kid named Faron Epps to play lead
guitar with us so we could have more variety in our numbers. Then we decided to find a girl singer for harmony, so
we had tryouts at the Wagon Wheel one Saturday mornin.
Me and Laverne and Arvell and Faron was there to decide if
any of the girls would fit in.

And the gals did parade through, most of em needin a
decongestant pill, a-singin all up in their noses, and making
big wet eyes. I reckon they figgered they's Kitty Wells, but
damned if most of em didn't sound like cats in heat. There
was some pretty ones, but after a dozen run through, I didn't
think we's gonna have no luck.

Then damned if a surprise didn't come. Ol Laverne he
poked me in the ribs and whispered, "Lookee yonder," just
after the front door opened and another girl come in. I
looked, and there stood the same pretty gal that had
whupped us in the talent contest at the picture show. And
old fat ass was with her. He right away blustered around
and demanded "Who's in charge here!" pokin at the air
with a cee-gar.

"I am," Arvell answered.

"Good," said ol Fatso, "I'm John J. Fergerberger,
Hollywood talent scout and theatrical agent. I'm prepared
to offer the services of Miss Sally Rolph, the well-known
starlet and singer, to your establishment if you can make
a satisfactory offer."

Arvell he looked at us, and I looked at the gal; damned
if she didn't look like she's about to bawl.

Arvell, he stood up and walked over the big-shot-dot-
the-oh, and he said: "I'll make ye a little offer. I *won't* kick
yer ass if ye git outa here right now. But if ye don't, I'm
a-gonna kick it right up between yer shoulder blades. Is that
satisfactory?"

John J. Fergerberger liked to swallowed his cee-gar.
"Huh?" he said.

Arvell just reached over and grabbed fat ass by the
collar and goosed him out of the door. "And now for you,
maam," he said to the girl, and she busted out bawlin, so
Arvell he held up.

I went over and put my arms around the girl, and she snuggled right up, little and a-whimperin, her big soft tits warm against my chest. I winked at Laverne. "Take er easy maam," I said, "Arvell didn't mean it, did you Arvell."

Arvell he looked pissed.

"Oh," the gal sobbed, "that man hasn't helped me a bit. He even took my prize money, and I just want to sing." Laverne winked at me, and I knowed he was a-thinkin money wasn't all ol John J. Fergerberger got off her; Laverne made me sore, him thinkin the same thing I was a-thinkin, what with me protectin her and all.

"Out!" hollered Arvell.

"Now wait a minute," I said. "This gal didn't do nothin." I felt my face gettin cold and somethin in my belly tightenin up.

Arvell he just looked at me. "We don't need her. Maybe ol furburger does."

That pissed me, him sayin "furburger" right in front of the poor gal. "Watch your mouth, Arvell," I warned him, and I wasn't kiddin none.

"You get out too," he said, "and take your whore with you…"

I reckon Arvell had more to say, but I caught him with a hell of a lick, knocked him on his butt. I'd of kicked a few of his rotten teeth out too if that damn Laverne hadn't grabbed me and roughed me up some, the son-of-a-bitch. "You ain't messin this job up for me," Laverne spit, but if I'd a been on top of him, I'd a messed up more than his job.

All the time, Sally she just screamed and howled. I guess opera folks don't see too many fights where they sing. There wasn't nothin for me to do but take her out into the parkin lot. Then's when I realized what I'd done, standin there next to the "Appearing Tonight: JESSIE & LAVERNE no cov. no min. dancing nightly" sign, and all of a sudden I felt like bawlin myownself. That's when Sally she calmed down and put her head on my shoulder and thanked me. Pissed as I was, I couldn't help but think of how hard me and Laverne had worked for that job, ever since we's in juvie up at Camp Owens years before. And it was gone that quick for a gal I didn't even know.

Well, I had the gal not the job by that time, and there wasn't no use cryin about it. At least I could try and get me a little piece. I knew that if I'd a crawled back into the Wagon Wheel and begged Arvell to let things slide and take me back again, he'd probably do it, since his audience come to see me much as Laverne, but there's no way in hell I's gonna apologize to that bastard. Naw, I just snuggled up to Sally and took her home with me.

Next day me and her worked on some duets—singin I mean—and Sally she really could. I figured what with me bein known and all, I could get us a job at one of the honky tonks out on Edison Highway or over in Oildale or maybe out to Taft. We worked on half-a-dozen songs, easy ones, me showin her how to yodel a little, and how to get that catch in her voice on ballads. She caught on real quick.

While we's practicin, Laverne called up and said that Arvell would take me back if I come and apologized. I told him Arvell could kiss my ass. He didn't say nothin for a while, then he told me he was sorry we'd got into it, specially over some silly woman. Well, ol Laverne's a good guy, but him saying that made me sore, so I told him he could kiss off too. He kindly spit over the phone that Arvell would black-ball me if I didn't come back, and I told him Arvell'd have some black balls if I ever got ahold of him again.

Me and Sally practiced for a couple days, workin on songs a feller and gal could sing that me and Laverne couldn't. Then on Wednesday the phone rang, and it's Larry Rose who managed the Kousin Ken T.V. show; he said I was canned. So I give him a little advice too. Ol Arvell sure hadn't wasted no time.

It took one hell of a lot of work to find any job at all, even though lots of guys wanted to hire us. I could tell. We drove by the Wagon Wheel and seen how the sign had been changed to read "Laverne and Faron." Finally, this little beer bar in Lamont, Okie Ed's, took us on for a small percentage of the nightly net. We liked to starved for awhile, but pretty soon we's packin em in ever night. Sally could really sing.

We lived in a little house over in Arvin by then. She's quite a gal, Sally; we hit it off real good, workin and playin.

The only thing that spoiled it was me wonderin about the
other guys that had had her, especially that raunchy old
Fergerberger. It really eat on me.

One night, just before we left Okie Ed's and moved up
in the world with a job at Woody Wright's Corral in Bakersfield, we finished a set and Sally said she needed to nap
before we went on again. I felt fresh, so I snuck out to the
bar for a beer and seen these two guys a-lookin at somethin
over in a corner booth near me. They's gigglin and carryin
on like queers, and I heard pieces of what they's sayin:
"Look at them tits! You wouldn't think they's real!" one
ol boy said. Then I heard the other one: "Hell, let's talk to
her after the show. She done it before; I bet we can get her
to do it again. She likes it, you can tell."

Somethin in me commenced tightenin cause I just
knew they's talkin about Sally, the sons-of-bitches. I walked
right up to em, and said: "What're you boys lookin at?"

Maybe they's drunk, but they never even looked nervous; one ol boy stared at me bold as a gopher snake, and
showed me two snapshots; "Your partner," he sneered. It

was Sally alright, naked and broke open and hot lookin in one photo, and worse in the other, a lot worse.

The tightness in me busted and I pushed their table hard up against em, pinnin them two bastards against the back of the booth, and really worked on em while they tried to get away. Okie Ed he said it was the worst beatin he ever seen one man give two, but it wasn't half of what I would a done. While they carted them two guys out, I picked up the photos and stuck em in my pocket. I's a-gonna show em to Sally and kick her ass out. I didn't need her, by God, and I didn't need my guts a-churnin up the way they were just a-thinkin of her and them pictures and things.

When we finally finished up that night and was drivin home, Sally asked me what was wrong; she said I'd been actin real cold toward her ever since that fight. I said me actin cold oughta be a relief, but she didn't get it. She asked me what I'd fought about, and I wanted to tell her right then, but the words wouldn't come out; my god damned lower lip kept quiverin on me, and my eyes felt all warm. But I was a-gonna throw her out, by God.

Then she said there was somethin she had to tell me and now was as good a time as any. She was pregnant with my baby and she wanted me to either marry her or let her have an abortion. That was all I needed. That really fucked things up. I just felt like a sack a turtle turds. What the hell could I do? No baby a mine was gettin abortioned if I could help it, and no baby a mine was growin up a bastard. But how the hell could Sally've got pregnant? I mean, if she's whorin around like the pictures showed, and she didn't, why now?

I burned them pictures and pissed on the ashes. Soon as our contract with Woody Wright run out, I got us an even better bookin up in Fresno. I didn't wanta be around Bakersfield no more, cause ever time I looked at the guys in the audience, I didn't know which ones had banged Sally and which hadn't. I didn't know who had copies of them pictures—and others, maybe—and who didn't. I just couldn't stand thinkin about it, with her carryin my baby and all. My belly got to hurtin, and I had to give up beer and commence drinkin milk all the time.

One evenin before we moved to Fresno, somethin hap-

pened that showed me again how much Jesus works in our
lives. Who should come in the Corral but John J. Fergerberger. Sally was in back, and the band was tunin up, while
I was puttin a new string on my guitar, sittin on the edge
of the stage. The front door busted open, and I heard the
voice demand "Where's the manager!"

"Right here," I hollered.

He come over, then said I wasn't no manager, but I'd
do for now. I felt myself gettin tight while he blabbed about
how he was Sally's manager and wantin his cut and how
he'd get a lawyer on me and that's when I ruined a good
acoustic guitar on his fat head. But I couldn't stop. I
stomped him so bad that Heavy, the bouncer, had to pull
me off. It was Jesus put Heavy there when He did, and I'm
grateful cause I believe I'd a killed Fergerberger. He had to
go to the hospital as it was, but for some reason he never
pressed charges or sued either.

Finally, after we moved to Fresno, and was married
and everything, Sally she brought things to a head. I guess
I'd been actin funny or some such, but I just couldn't forgive her, or even tell her why I was sore. I couldn't stand
to get close to her after seein those pictures to kiss her or
even touch her. She come to me and said I'd changed and
was makin life mighty rough on her, her bein pregnant and
all, and that if I didn't love her she'd rather have our baby
in a gutter. She said she'd conceived the baby with love,
but now she knew I was just play-actin and she wasn't goin
to lead that kind of life. I almost told her off right then, but
somethin in me got all warm and soft.

I didn't know what to say. A man can't love a woman
that done what Sally had, but I couldn't stand to lose her
either, not to mention the baby. Maybe if I told what I knew
about her she'd be humbled and beg me to forgive her, but
then I couldn't forgive her because she'd know I knew.
Oh Lord.

Sally had commenced packing, a-cryin to herself, and I
just stood there like a cow in quicksand, not knowin what
to do but sink. I closed my eyes and just prayed, my belly
a-boilin, and Jesus he reminded me of Mary Magdalene;
Jesus never let me down yet.

"Sally," I finally was able to say, "I need you, honey.

Don't leave. I'll make things right again." I put my arms around her and kissed her, and pretty soon my belly didn't hurt. But I couldn't lie and say I loved her, cause a man just can't love a woman who's whored. I sure as hell wasn't lyin when I told her I couldn't live without her, though; I really couldn't. And that shows how clever Jesus works, too, cause He had me apologizin when she was the guilty one.

It wasn't long after that night we commenced singin sacred songs at the Full Gospel Tabernacle, just before our first son, Laverne Jessie, was born. Then we quit singin in barrooms altogether. And it was right after Laverne Jessie's birth that we got discovered and made our first golden record in Nashville. Maybe you heard it. It's called "What A Friend We Have In Jesus."

For Lionel Williams

Compañeros

Through the truck's open back, canvas fly flapping in cool morning breeze, a faint pale blue glow broke over the distant Sierra Nevadas. Men and boys crouched or squatted or sat on the truck's bouncing floor, some snoring, others talking in hushed voices, many in Spanish. A bottle of Thunderbird was passed by three older Okie men; two splibs shared a short dog of white port.

Near the back of the truck's bed six high school football players clustered, telling stories, giggling, exaggerating their exploits as fighters or athletes or lovers. Quincy Williams, the only black in the group poked Chava, the thick-necked Chicano sitting next to him. "Watch this," he said, leaning then toward the two older Negroes passing the white port bottle. "Say brother," Quincy crooned, "that pluck sure do look fine. You ain't got a little taste for me do you?" He smiled.

One older man turned his red-rimmed eyes toward Quincy. "Say what?" he replied thickly.

"A little taste, brother," Quincy repeated, a hint of demand sneaking into his voice. He sensed eyes on him now, and tingling exhilaration suddenly grew within him.

Both older black men looked at him, unmoving, one holding the little bottle of white port in a large, calloused hand. "Ain't this a bitch," he chuckled. "Young pup want growed-up dog food." Many older men laughed.

"And he gonna jump bad," added the other Negro.

Quincy's exhilaration slowly melted into tension flecked with fear as human silence filled the jostling, rattling truck.

It was his move. Outside, through flapping canvas, faint
yellow began to show over the far-away mountains. "Gimme
a taste, man," he heard himself say, his voice cracking as
he tried to give it a hard edge. More laughter sprinkled
the men.

"Better watch out there, Willie," he heard an old Okie
croak to the man holding the bottle, "that little ol' boy's
a-fixin' to tell his momma on ya!" A wave of laughter.

"I already *knows* his momma," Willie replied. Laughter
again, louder. The thick-necked Mexican sitting next to
Quincy said to him quietly, "Cool it, ese." None of the other
high school boys spoke or moved.

"Cool shit!" Quincy shouted, his voice turned frantic.
"I'll make these motherfuckers sorry they got in my family!"

"Calmese bato," the Mexican repeated, his own voice
tense, yet authoritative, nodding toward Willie's drinking
companion who now held a straight-edged razor wound with
friction tape in one hand close to his side. Quincy stared
momentarily, quivering with fear and rage, then allowed
himself to be pulled back by Chava; "Calmese un ratito."

Tension broken, murmuring rose again as though
nothing had happened, and workers mumbled their way to
the fields, the truck turning onto a dirt lane. Rows of staked

grape vines could be seen on both sides of the road out the truck's back, then a large farm yard and aluminum barn, then cotton. The truck jerked to a halt, and workers swung slowly out.

Already other truckloads of workers had emptied, and bent figures could be seen moving through dusty rows. A cotton-picking machine had earlier stripped the field; now people would earn their living by picking what it missed. "Damn," one stringy white man said, "ol Strawberry Jim went and got us here late again." Strawberry Jim—a freckled, redhaired Negro—owned the truck and acted as crew pusher. The truck was his source of income, the truck and the folks he gathered to pick or weed or sow; most men that morning were regular members of his crew.

Only one of the six boys—Chava—was an experienced field hand, though they had all worked in packing sheds during the summer. They had decided to work this Saturday more as a lark than to make much money, still each claimed he could pick more cotton than any of the others. They played football for the championship team at the high school in East Bakersfield, but San Joaquin Valley sun and tough cotton bolls didn't read sport sections. Neither did Strawberry Jim.

"Was that one a you boys make trouble in the back?" he asked them as they lined up to sign-in and draw their sacks. His eyes searched each of them, pausing on the deep brown face of All-League Player of the Year, Quincy Williams, who avoided him. The boys all looked away or at their feet, all except Chava and a lean blond named Jerrall.

"Naw," Jerrall answered with a grin, "just some kiddin' around there, chief."

Strawberry Jim remained unconvinced. "Anymore bullshit and you-all be walkin' home."

"Walk home!" the blond boy exclaimed with a warm laugh. "Man, that's gotta be fifteen miles."

Strawberry remained grim. "All a that," he said.

The boys drew their sacks and walked to their rows; they put the sacks' straps over their shoulders, then began pulling at sinewy cotton plants, stooping, beheading them with quick jerks, tossing the dusty white bolls into the long

sacks that dangled behind like tadpole tails. Although it
was fall, a fierce sun burst over the distant mountains and
burnt their exposed necks and heads; they turned collars
up and tied handkerchiefs over hot scalps.

Their lower backs soon ached and their hands grew
prickly numb. They fell steadily behind the rest of the crew,
even the old winoes, trying hard to compete but seeing the
oldtimers outdistancing them, they began making a joke
of it, secretly believing the others would tire soon and they
would catch and pass them. "Holy Christ," said Raymie,
whose fair skin led most people to assume he was anything
but a Chicano, standing and rubbing his sore back, "look
at them guys. They're clear up to Delano." Everyone
laughed.

Jerrall asked what time it was; "I'm ready for lunch,"
he said.

"Nine-o'clock," answered Manuel. His brother, Julio,
working the row next to him sighed a desperate "Hijole!"

A few minutes later Jerrall stood, rubbed his stiffening
back, "How much money you reckon we made so far?" he
asked the group.

Chava grunted, but Quincy laughed, saying: "Sheeit,
you ain't picked but a dime so far."

"Hell, I got more than you do!" Jerrall answered
quickly.

"Sheeit!"

Chava straightened-up, looked at Jerrall's sack, then
Quincy's. "Neither one of you even got a lump in your sacks
yet," he finally said. "You payosos need a heuvos a lo
Chicano." Raymie, Manuel and Julio laughed.

Just as Jerrall prepared a verbal counter-punch, he
noticed Strawberry Jim striding toward them through waist-
high cotton. "Here comes the man," he barked. They all
snapped back into action, but in a moment Strawberry
stopped them.

"I done foretold you-all I don't want no bullshit. Now
catch-up with the crew or start doin' you road work. I ain't
carryin' nothin' but workin' mens in my truck. You-all ain't
hit a lick yet."

Jerrall smiled. "We're just gettin' warmed-up, chief,"

he responded pleasantly. "Wait'll that sun gets up and starts
to meltin' all them old farts. Then you'll see who the real
workers are. Don't worry."

"I ain't worried for me, boy. I worried for you-all. You
boys don't start doin' a better job, you be walkin'. Looky
down them rows. You-all leave more cotton than you pick.
Hell, I seen one little bitty Flip could pick more than you-
all." He spit disdainfully past the damp cigar butt that
stained his pink lips. "One dried-up Flip."

After nervous laughter from the other boys, Chava, un-
smiling, said: "Alivianese chavalo bravoso. We can't pick
nothing with you in the way, puto."

"Don't talk none a that shit to me, boy!"

"Simón, cabrón," whispered Manuel.

Raymie, seeing Chava's black eyes suddenly blaze, his
neck swell, stepped between his friend and Strawberry Jim.
"We just wanta work, guy. No offense."

"You're the man," Jerrall added.

"You damn right I the man. I carry you-all out here.
Damn right. And no bullshit either!" Strawberry whirled
and strode angrily toward the road.

"Take it easy, Chava," Raymie cautioned. "Les va
llegar su tiempo," he said. "It's no big deal to whip an old
bastard like Straw, but it's a hell of a long walk home."
Chava said nothing, but began tearing cotton from stalks
and thrusting it into the sack draped over his shoulder.

But the others soon forgot Strawberry Jim's warning.
They were still falling steadily behind the older pickers
despite renewed effort; soon their zeal gave way to humor.
Quincy called to Jerrall: "Hey Okie, dig!" he dropped a
potato-sized rock into his sack; "That's a dime right there,"
he said. All but Chava laughed. A moment later Manuel held
an even larger stone; "I got a quarter's worth," he boasted.
Soon they were all tossing rocks, then clods, into their
sacks, laughing.

At the end of their long rounds, the boys dragged their
sacks first to the water can where they drank, their blistered
hands stiff, their humor thinning. "What time is it now?"

"Half-past."

"Half-past what?"

"Half-past ten."

"Shit!"

Then they trudged to the big spring-scale hanging from an open-bedded truck. Strawberry Jim squatted in the shade of the cab talking to other pushers, while two of the farmer's men—one a husky Chicano, the other a ruddy-faced Italian—weighed and tallied the sacks. "Thirty-nine," the Chicano barked as Chava's sack was weighed. Jerrall was next; "Thirty-eight," the Chicano shouted, giving Jerrall a strange look. Manuel's weighed thirty-nine pounds, and the Chicano said rapidly to him: "Esta maderiando." Manuel shrugged. Julio looked away when the man at the scale shouted "Thirty-one."

Quincy hung his sack on the scale's hook. "Oh bullshit!" they heard Strawberry Jim cry from where he'd been watching them. "That sack ain't got no fifty pounds in it!" Quincy's rich brown face bleached suddenly to the color of dust. "You ain't weighin'," he replied lamely.

The red-faced Wop looked-up from his tally sheet. "How much rock you got in there, huh?"

Quincy tried to clear his throat. "Rock?" he finally managed to say.

The Wop kicked Quincy's sack; it sounded like a kid's bag of marbles. "Mofuckah!" Strawberry Jim exclaimed.

"This ain't quarry work," the Wop said.

Quincy looked from his accusers to his pals, who avoided his eyes. "I must of accidently got a few rocks in there." He felt as though everything, even the sky, was congealing around him, choking him. He felt absolutely alone.

"My ass!" Strawberry Jim chanted with glee. "Nigger, you canned. Get you black booty outa here!"

A weakness sucked at Quincy. He wanted to flatten that loudmouth Strawberry, but instead he only looked toward the Wop, who affirmed his firing: "He's the crewpusher."

"Aw, man," Quincy said weakly, "we only jivin'."

"You be jivin'," Strawberry laughed. "Now get gone."

The Wop kicked Jerrall's bag, then Manuel's, Raymie's, and Julio's. "All the same," he reported; only Chava's bag passed inspection. "What are you jokers tryin' to pull?"

"Fire they asses, Guido," Strawberry prompted. "They troublemakers."

A tiny Filipino, his hair an oily burst of black glory, suddenly spoke up. "No work. Alla time pluck alound. No good."

"See," Strawberry added, "don't take Flip no time to see they jive-asses."

The Wop finally asked them why they bothered to come out to the field if they didn't intend to work. Jerrall tried to talk their way out of it, but got nowhere. Other workers, including Willie and his razor-toting friend, sensing trouble, gathered around the boys. A leathery old Okie asked "What's up, Straw?"

"These boys be puttin' rocks in they sacks."

The old man shook his head; he turned to Jerrall and said quietly: "You boys shore fucked-up. Don't ya know the boss'll give ya a few rocks and not say nothin'. But, Christ, he cain't stand no screwin'." The old man wandered away to the water can and Jerrall wished he was with him. Willie and his friend just grinned. The Filipino bounced next to them like a shadow-boxer.

"You-all ain't riding back to town in my truck; at least none of you but him," he nodded toward Chava.

Chava's swollen neck seemed to pulse as he answered. "We're all together, cabrón."

"You lettin' him do this to us?" Jerrall demanded of the Wop.

"I'm not stoppin' him. You just stay out of my field."

Workers continued gathering. A wall of sweating pickers lined-up with the Wop. "These folks come out here to work and you-all come to play," Strawberry shouted, glancing around him at the growing group, feeling the power of increasing numbers, feeling current pass from man to man. "Now get you asses outa here."

The boys, all except Chava, had backed up several steps. Jerrall asked, "What about our pay?"

"No pay for rocks," the Wop responded, his own voice rising with excitement.

"My uncle's a lawyer, by God," Jerrall shouted sud-

denly, "he'll have your asses. You lousy sons-of-bitches."
His fists were clenched and he quivered as he yelled.

The crew closed around them and Chava turned, grab-
bing Jerrall's arm. "We're going," he said. Then he stopped,
turned, and stared at Strawberry Jim, fierce Indian eyes
glowing: "I'll be seeing *you* later, puto," Chava said. "Te
voy ha tener que chingar!"

Strawberry laughed uneasily, looking around him to
again check the strength of his numbers. When the boys
were out of earshot he said "Lazy mofuckahs," then went
about his business.

Noon roasted them when they found an irrigation ditch
full of clear, cold water. They lay on their bellies or knelt
and drank from cupped hands. They had decided to walk
home on dirt farm roads rather than Highway 99 because
they figured it would be shorter; they figured wrong. Their
sandwiches and burritos were long since eaten and their
feet burned.

"How far we come?" Raymie asked.

"Five miles, I guess," Jerrall answered.

"We could have stayed home and messed around, but
oh no, old Jerrall says we can get rich picking cotton," said
Raymie, shaking his head.

"Ol' Jerrall! Hell, I never said nothing about it. It was
Manuel's idea."

"Chinge su madre," Manuel replied, pumping his arms.
"Why don't you call your uncle the lawyer and sue me."

Jerrall had to laugh. "That scared 'em a little, anyway,"
he said.

"Te aventaste," Julio said sarcastically.

"Besides," Jerrall continued, ignoring Julio, "Quincy's
the one got us in dutch. First he starts a fight in the truck,
then he puts rocks in his sack."

"What were those things in your sack, man? Gold
nuggets?"

"Yeah, but you started it."

"Oh, go to hell. Don't pass go, don't collect no two
hundred dollars. You always whining about something.
Damn Okies ain't nothing but crybabies. Just like old Flip

say, 'Alla time cly, cly.' "

Everyone laughed. Manuel was suddenly burlesquing a Filipino, his voice high and stacatto: "We go chickee fights. Big blondie. Make pluck-pluck alla time." He did an awkward bump-and-grind. More laughter.

"And ol' Quincy really backed them two old boys down," Jerrall chortled. "That one guy would a sliced your throat so fast you'd had to shake your head to find out it was cut off."

"Sheeit, that's an old one." Quincy said, but he was laughing.

Only Chava remained sullen; his neck still swollen with anger, he looked like a copper-skinned toad squatting next to the irrigation ditch. "What's wrong, ese?" Raymie finally asked him.

"That damn Strawberry," Chava said, "he's gonna be one sorry mayate."

"Sheeit, he ain't no mayate," Quincy said indignantly. "He more Okie than anything. Just look at that red hair and freckles. Man, he probably old Jerrall's uncle."

Everyone—even Chava—chuckled.

"He's probably your daddy," Jerrall snapped.

"Don't get in my family, man," Quincy said with mock menace.

Two o'clock and they seemed no nearer home, trudging a burning dirt track through a grape field. There was no convenient water, no shade. "We shoulda walked the highways," Manuel moaned, "this isn't getting us nowhere."

"Hell," answered Jerrall, "it's too late to turn back now."

Their conversations dried-up with their throats as they straggled along. Before them the field shimmered in heat-waves. From overhead they heard the puttering engine of a small airplane. Jerrall looked up. "Piper Cub," he reported, not because he saw the plane, but because it was the only name he knew.

Twice, three times, pick-up trucks bounced past them toward town, enveloping them in clouds of choking dust, not even slowing down. "Aw, shit," Raymie moaned. They

broke clear of the grapes and entered a large flat tract of disked, unseeded land. Far across the tract they saw another dust cloud approaching them very fast, apparently from the highway; they couldn't see what kind of vehicle it was and didn't really care, for it was traveling in the wrong direction. Heads down, they continued trudging until Julio said softly, "That's a cop car or something." They all looked at it now, bearing down on them, an unmarked gray sedan. "La jura," Manuel said, his voice suddenly an octave higher. Chava grunted. The others looked with interest, but no apparent concern.

They parted and stood on the sides of the road to allow the speeding car to pass, but it screeched to a halt next to them. Two officers—Deputy Sheriffs—jumped from the car and examined them with pale eyes, then the older officer ordered: "You, you, and you. Over here." The younger officer stood next to the gray car, his right hand resting lightly on his service revolver while his partner showed Julio and Manuel and Chava where to stand. "You got papers?" the older sheriff asked without smiling. Stunned silence. "Papers?" he repeated, louder this time.

Jerrall, recovering from his initial shock, dug his bony elbow into Quincy's ribs. "Giff me your bapers," he whispered, one eye squinting as though holding a monocle. "You are a chew?"

"What's that?" snapped the older officer.

"Nothin'...ah, sir," Jerrall answered.

"All right, hit the car," ordered the officer, and the three Chicanos were forced to lean onto the car with their legs spread while they were searched. Julio and Manuel looked frightened; Chava stared sullenly ahead.

"That's right, officer," Jerrall whispered out the side of his mouth to Quincy, "search them dangerous criminals."

As their parents had advised, the boys had left their wallets at home, bringing only social security cards. "Where'd you get these?" the sheriff asked after directing them to stand next to the car once again. For a moment no one answered, then Chava asked: "Where'd you get yours?"

"What are you, a wise guy. Answer the question."

"At the social security office in Bakersfield," Manuel said.

"Not you," barked the officer, "him." He nodded at Chava.

"The same place you got yours," Chava said.

Across the car's gray roof the two officers exchanged looks. "I think this one's a alien," the older sheriff said.

"Alien my berga," Chava spat. "My people were in California when yours were still screwing Indians in Oklahoma." He lunged at the sheriff. With astounding swiftness there was a wet *crack!* The officer sapped him. Chava sagged, caught himself, threw a short powerful punch that bounced off the officer's mouth; he was sapped again and fell to one knee, where he was again sapped and finally collapsed. Raymie, his fair skin suddenly purple with rage, leapt toward the officer who stood over Chava, shouting "Pongale hijo de la chingada, you punk bastard!" But the silent younger sheriff had unholstered his revolver; he leveled it at Raymie and the others. "Back up," he warned.

"Us too?" asked Manuel, his voice quavering.

"All of you."

They backed into the field, while Chava was handcuffed and loaded—thrown like an empty cotton sack—into the backseat of the car. Then the older man dropped the Social Security cards onto the road. His lip was bloody and swelling. He daubed at it with an ironed handkerchief as he told

them he had acted in self-defense and not to forget it. "Get
the hell home and don't let me find any of you"—he was
glaring at Raymie who returned his glare—"in my area
again."

The sheriff's car buzzed away in a cloud of fine tan
dust, and the boys stood in the field watching it disappear,
looking then at one another.

"Jesus," Quincy muttered, "that old man *bad.*"

"They hire 'em bad," Manuel replied weakly.

"That Chava baddest, though," Quincy went on.
"Sheeit, man, he fight anything."

"Tiene mucho huevos," Julio said in a quiet, tense
voice, faintly ashamed, "...mucho hombre."

"Those bastards!" Raymie growled.

The five boys trudged on, finally reaching the outskirts
of Bakersfield: small, old farms with collapsing chicken
houses, occasional alfalfa fields, nondescript horses in un-
whitewashed corrals, and barren oil fields to the east. "At
least Chava got a ride to town," Jerrall offered, but no one
laughed.

Chava's father paid his son's fine and obtained his
release from the security section of the county hospital.
Chava had been placed there after it was discovered he had
broken ribs, apparently when he fell down steps at the
county jail. At least that's what the official report said, and
Chava's father didn't bother to question the report.

48

Cowboys

This old boy named Shorty Moore used to haul mud out to
the rig, see. Shorty he could whup a man and he never
ducked a fight, so not many guys in the oilfields ever give
him much trouble.

One time old Shorty he was sitting around the doghouse at quitting time while us guys changed to go home,
and this engineer looked at Shorty's duds, then asked
Shorty real smart alecky if he was a cowboy. All of us on
the crew just set back to watch Shorty stomp the bastard,
see, but old Shorty he fooled us. He looked around, kind of
grinned, and said real quiet: Naw, I ain't no cowboy. Never
have been. But I wear these boots and this belt and shirt
because they're western, see, working men's clothes. And
I feel western. I ain't no college sissy with a necktie and
pink hands. I'm a man and that's what my clothes say. Any
old boy that doubts it ain't got but to jump and I'll kick his
ass for him.

That was that. The engineer never said nothing more,
so old Shorty just let things slide and I guess everyone was
happy to get out of the doghouse that afternoon.

But, you know, everytime a guy turns around in
Bakersfield some pasty-faced bastard's eyeing your belt
buckle or boots, and you just know he's a-thinking *cowboy*
and laughing at you to hisself. They all think they're high
powers. I ain't like old Shorty; things like that just eat on
me. I work as hard as any man does for my wages, a-bucking
pig iron on a drilling rig, and I can't take some pencil-necked

fairy that works in a office looking down his nose at me.
I'll break his nose for him, by God.

Last summer whenever the college kids come out to
replace guys going on vacation, wouldn't you know we'd
get us a hippy. And it was comical as hell when this kid first
drove up to the rig. We'd just spudded in, see, a-hoping to
hit gas on Suisun Bay up near Fairfield. It was tower change
and my crew was working daylights. About the time we
walked out of the doghouse, and old Turk Brown's crew
was coming off, see, up sputters this little red sports car
with a great big long-haired kid a-driving it. Well, he gets
out of the car, all the guys just kind of standing back watching him, and he commences talking to the pusher. That kid

was so huge, and his car was so small, he looked like a big
old snake coming out of a little basket: more and more of
him kept coming after you just knew the car couldn't hold
no more.

Old Arkie Williams he made a kissing sound with his
mouth and the kid looked at him. I seen cold eyes before,
but that kid looked like he could put a fire out staring at it.
And I could see that even though Arkie kept on bullshitting,
he knew he made a mistake. Is it a boy or a girl? Arkie said.
He never did have enough sense to admit he was wrong
after he started spouting off. The pusher told us to get up
on the rig and pull them slips, and the kid was still just
a-looking at Arkie, not saying nothing; I figured Arkie was
into it. Too bad for him too. He never could fight a lick.

The kid went to work that morning and spent the
whole tower helping Buford Kileen clean out the pumps.
Come quitting time, we all headed for the doghouse hot to
get changed and go drink us some beer. Just about the time
Arkie walked up to the doorway from between pipe racks,
the new kid stepped in front of him and bam! one punch
cold cocked him. Jesus, could that big old kid punch! And
that ain't all; Arkie hadn't but hit the ground and the kid
had him kicked three or four times. We grabbed the kid and
had one hell of a time holding him while two boys from the
crew that was just coming to work helped Arkie. The pusher
took the kid into his office and told him, I guess, any more
fighting and he'd be canned. And the pusher took Arkie
aside and told him he'd got just what he deserved.

What really got me though was that the new kid never
said nothing. After it was over he just got out of his work
clothes and climbed into suede drawers with fringes on 'em,
and high cowboy boots, and a western belt with a big tur-
quois buckle. He put on some little colored beads and a
leather sombrero and out he walked, no shirt at all. He
climbed into his little red car, see, and drove off without
saying goodbye or kiss my ass or nothing.

After he was gone some of the guys commenced
kidding about the high falutin cowboy clothes the kid wore.
I'll bet he never rode nothing but that little red car, old
Buford said, cept maybe a few of them college coeds. Every-

one laughed. Yeah, Easy Ed Davis said, he's a real cow-
poke that one, must think he's Buffalo Bill with that long
hair. Reckon we ought to buy him some ribbons to go with
them beads? I asked. Arkie never laughed, then pretty soon
he ups and says that if the kid ever messed with him again,
by God, there'd be one more cowboy on Boot Hill. Shorty
Moore showed up a little later at this beer joint where we
usually went, and he said he didn't have no use for hippies
period. No use a-tall.

The kid turned out to be one hell of a worker; he give
a honest jump for his wages, I'll say that much. He never
let none of the boys on the job get real friendly with him,
but he seemed to like it when they commenced calling him
Cowboy. He didn't know that most of the guys wanted to
call him Dude, but they thought better of it. He was a big
old boy.

I could tell he really didn't give a damn for none of us.
Whenever he did talk to us it was to show off all of his book
learning and to hint at how ignorant he figured we was.
You know, one of us might say he thought the Dodgers
would go all the way this year, and young Cowboy would
kind of sneer: It all depends on whether they can exploit
more blacks than the other teams, he'd say, shit like that.
Hell, he couldn't stand to see us enjoy nothing; he liked to
wreck things for everyone it seemed like. Cowboy was
studying to be a college pro-fessor and he had about that
much sense.

A couple of months after he first come to work, we
finally lifted the kid. He was tougher than most summer
hires to trick because he didn't talk much, and he didn't
seem to give a damn about what we thought of him. But old
Easy Ed, our derrick man, he finally bullshitted the kid into
it. Easy Ed could talk a nigger white if you give him half
a chance. He just kept a-gabbing at Cowboy all the time, see,
telling him he didn't know what a strong man was. Hell,
old Ed would say, a young buck like you ain't seen a stout
man till you seen a old timer like me hot after it. There ain't
many old boys in this oil patch can lift as much weight as
me, by God. I can pick up three guys at one time. Easy Ed's
just a little bitty fart, and the kid would kind of look at him

funny but not say nothing. It was comical, really. Cowboy would bring all these books with him to read when he ate, but he'd no more than get his dinner bucket open than Easy Ed would be a-chewing on his ear. I believe that kid finally give in just to shut Ed up.

We was circulating mud and waiting for the engineers to give us the go ahead on making more hole that day; everyone was pretty bored. We'd just finished unloading sacks of chemicals off Shorty's truck, and we was kind of laying around on the mud rack chewing tobacco and telling lies. Pretty soon up comes Easy Ed and he right away starts in on Cowboy. Before long the kid said O.K., let's see you lift three guys.

So everybody trooped around behind the rig, and old Ed laid down a length of rope on the ground. Then he said: three of you boys lay down on her. Heavy, he said to me, you take one side. Shorty you take the other. Cowboy, you crawl in the middle. I want you to know there ain't no trick to it. We three got down on our backs while the other guys stood around us. Ed just kept a-jabbering, see. I swear, that guy should of been a preacher; he damn sure could of talked some sisters into the bushes.

Well, anyways, old Ed tells us three to wrap our arms and legs around each other (me and Shorty knowing this stuff from way back, but not letting on, so the kid won't suspect nothing). Now make her real tight, Ed tells us, I don't want nobody slipping when I pick y'all up. Me and Shorty really cinched up on the kid's arms and legs, see. We had him pinned to the ground and I could tell he was catching on.

Ed, a-yacking all the time, commenced unbottoning Cowboy's fly and Buford handed Ed the dope brush. The kid tensed up, then kind of chuckled and relaxed. Ah shit, he said, laughing a little, I figured then it was gonna be a easy lifting, and that the kid wasn't half bad after all. But just about the time Easy Ed started painting the kid's balls with dope, old Arkie couldn't keep his mouth shut. He kind of spit at the kid: In the position you let us get you in, weavil, just thank of all the thangs we *could* do to you. Then he made that kissing sound.

Oh Jesus! The kid just exploded! I'm a pretty stout old boy myownself, see, but Cowboy just sort of shook me loose, then kicked Ed in the slats with his free foot. I've helped lift maybe a hundred weavils in my day, and nobody never just shook me off before. Old Shorty hung on and in a minute the two of them was rolling around in the dust and puncture vines. Shorty don't know how to give up in a fight, and he held on to that big old boy like a dog on a bull.

We knew the pusher would can the kid if he seen him fighting, so we all jumped in and broke her up. When we managed to get them apart, the kid's eyes locked on Shorty, and Shorty he stuck his finger in the kid's face and said: Name the place Cowboy. We'll finish her where there ain't nobody gonna get in the way. The kid just kept staring and said anyplace was fine with him.

There was this little beer joint at a eucalyptus grove between where we was drilling and Rio Vista. That's where Shorty and the kid decided to meet after work. The whole crew drove right over there and drank beer while they waited for Shorty to get back from Lodi where he left his truck in the chemical company's yard every evening. The kid he stayed outside a-leaning on his little red car, see, his sombrero tilted back, his long hair a-blowing in the wind. Them frozen blue eyes of his just glowed. Damned if he

don't look like some oldtime gunfighter, Buford said looking
out the window. I told him that was one cowboy I didn't
want to tangle with. You notice he never messes with me
no more, Arkie bragged, and all the guys laughed, but old
Arkie was serious and he didn't see nothing funny. Naturally, Easy Ed took to laying bets: I taken old Shorty, he
said, and I'll put five bucks on him. Buford covered him
right away. Arkie bet on Shorty too, and Buford covered
him. Ain't you a-betting Heavy? Ed asked me, but I said
no. I didn't feel too good about the whole thing.

Shorty drove up directly and crawled out of his Chevy.
For a minute him and Cowboy just stood there staring at
each other, then Cowboy he bent over and reached into his
car and pulled out a gunbelt, the old kind with ammunition
loops and long thongs dangling from the holster. He slipped
her on and tied the thongs around his right thigh. Hey! I
heard Buford say and when I looked away from the kid, I
seen old Shorty was doing the same thing.

All of us guys froze where we was. Cowboy and Shorty
they pulled their six-guns from the holsters, spun the cylin-
ders and kinda blew on the sights. Then they slid the
revolvers back into leather and commenced walking toward
one another. What the hell is this? Easy Ed whispered, but
I couldn't answer, my heart was a-stompin inside my chest
and I couldn't even swallow. I wanted to holler, but I just
stood there.

When they was about twenty-five or thirty feet apart—
real close—Cowboy and Shorty stopped, then spread their
legs like they was gonna pick up somethin heavy. It's yer
play, dude, Shorty said, his eyes pointed straight at Cowboy's. Cowboy he kinda rocked back on his heels: You've
been alive too long, he croaked. You've out-lived yourself.

Then the roar! In what seemed like a forever of sound,
they dipped their right shoulders and threw their right hands
straight down. There wasn't no fancy grabbin and wingin,
movie-style, just two short, efficient moves, like when a
good worker shovels.

And Shorty busted backwards, almost up in the air,

then fell in a heap, a puppet without strings, empty, his gun in the dirt. A cloud of blue smoke hung where he'd stood.

Oh sweet lovin Jesus! I cried out, and I run over to Shorty, but he'd had it. He was all sprawled out, his eyes looking like egg-whites. Little frothy bubbles was coming from his brisket, but not much blood. He coughed, choked maybe, and a gusher shot up from his mouth and from the hole in his middle, then the bubbles quit.

Get your ass away from him, I heard Cowboy say. I looked at the kid. He still held his six-gun, and the blue smoke still hung there in front of him; there wasn't no wind. I looked back down at Shorty and seen a great big puddle of blood was growing underneath him, peekin out, not red but kinda maroon, almost black. Get! Cowboy hollered again, so I walked back to where the other boys stood. I couldn't do old Shorty no good.

Cowboy holstered his pistol, untied the thong, then slipped the gunbelt off and dropped it into his car. You guys gonna buy me a beer? he asked. None of us said nothing. I didn't figure so, he said. He climbed into his car, backed up—me afraid he was agonna run over Shorty but he was real careful not to—then started out onto the road. Then he done something real funny; he slowed down, almost stopped, and flashed us one of them V-peace signs hippies are always makin. He drove away toward Fairfield, up over a low hill into the fading sun.

Jesus, Buford said, what're we gonna do?

Easy Ed he just kept lookin from where Shorty lay with a big old blow-fly already doin business on his bloody lower lip, then back toward the hill where Cowboy'd disappeared. We might could form a posse, he said.

Passage

Mrs. Sandrini bought Garth the gun. Mother and Dad said he'd have to earn his own money come summer if he wanted one, he recalled years later, but Mrs. Sandrini could never tell him no. On his tenth birthday she had presented him with a glistening Daisy air rifle, the BB gun he'd always wanted. And he'd been happy, even though Dad had lectured him for a solid hour on safety rules.

Since Dad was foreman at Mrs. Sandrini's farm, he didn't tell Garth he had to return the rifle, though that certainly would have suited Dad; a boy ought to earn what he wants, he told Mother, so he'll know its real worth. If you give a kid too much you cheat him. Mother just said Garth was too young for a gun, but the boy remembered Dad telling about using a shotgun himself when he was only ten.

Garth had known as soon as Mrs. Sandrini's pick-up stopped in front of the house and she had stepped out carrying the long package, he'd known his countless hints had borne fruit. Mother and Dad had known too. Their own gifts for him—a new Cub Scout shirt and a regulation pocket knife—seemed suddenly of no importance in the boy's flush of joy at owning an air rifle.

He had wanted to take it outside immediately, but by the time Dad had lectured him supper was ready. Darkness engulfed them as they ate, so his first shooting was postponed until the next day. He fondled the oily rifle all that evening and fell asleep with it beside him in bed. When Mother and Dad looked in on him before turning in themselves, they were surprised at how large he'd grown, and how old he looked stretched out next to his rifle. And they were a little sad.

Breakfast was a chore. Dad, of course, had long since driven from Wasco to Sandrini's farm. Mother insisted Garth eat a good breakfast, wondering aloud if he shouldn't wait to try his gun until Dad returned home from work: Daddy can show you how, she'd said. I know how already, he'd insisted, telling her about Bob Howard's rifle and how he'd hit a target using it.

In his pocket was twenty-five cents he'd earned mowing a neighbor's lawn. He had to walk to the dimestore to buy a package of ammunition. He knew exactly where to look in the store, but was forced to decide between a small cylinder of bright, copper-coated ammunition, or a larger packet of lead BB's. Both cost a dime. After considerable lip-biting deliberation, he purchased the larger packet of BB's and hurried home.

Mother again urged that he wait until his father returned before testing the gun but Garth prevailed. Outside,

he filled his mouth with cold shot, then blew them into the
rifle's ammunition chamber as he'd seen other boys do.
Then he extracted a stub pencil from one of his bulging
pockets and drew a target on a cardboard box in the back-
yard. He placed the box against one wall of the shed, positioned himself, and began to plunk away with his wheezing
weapon.

Try as he might, he couldn't seem to hold the front
sight steady and, once or twice, he missed the box com-
pletely and snapped rounds into the shed's unpainted wall.
He finally found that by lying on his belly and bracing his
arms he could hit the target consistently. There was nothing
to it. He sensed that Mother was watching him through a
back window, and felt coldly professional as he positioned
himself and sent another round into the box.

Reloading, he heard the pesty mockingbird that always
harassed their cat. I'll knock that old bird right out of the
chinaberry tree, he mused, beginning a big-game hunter's
stalk that left him with only the bird's disdainful Haw-Haw!
as it screeched away. He pulled a shot off at it, but wasn't
even close.

Then he heard the metallic song of another bird from
the neighbor's large sycamore tree and he stopped, staring
into the mass of nearly leafless branches until he spotted a
large robin challenging the day from a nearby perch. Without thinking, Garth locked his eyes on the bright-chested
bird. He crept closer, finally bracing his rifle on a rose trellis
and aiming. The bird was in the middle of his sights, its
proud breast thrust forward, its dark eyes like tiny beads of
life. Save for a curious cocking of its head, the bird did not
move. A strange warmth welled in Garth, an electric excitement; almost without realization, he squeezed the trigger,
felt the mild recoil against his shoulder, saw the bird hop,
hesitate, then tumble to the ground.

Garth did not change position for a long moment. Then
he realized what had happened. I got it! he thought joyfully.
I really got it! Sprinting to the tree, he could only imagine
Dad and Mother's surprise when they saw what he'd been
able to do. He was startled to find the robin very much
alive, flopping frantically on the grass. Its orange breast

seemed to have shrunk and it was smeared with bright blood. The bird was small and helpless, not the proud beast he had sighted in the tree. He watched its panicky dance around the base of the sycamore, confused, before the full impact of what he'd done struck him.

Oh no, he thought, I didn't want to hurt the bird, just to shoot it. And now it's bleeding. He dropped his rifle, tears beginning to fill his eyes, and chased the wounded bird until he caught it and picked it up, ignoring the jabs and nips of its yellow beak.

Running toward home, he called for Mother, who met him on the back porch. Momma, he cried, it's hurt! I didn't mean to, but I hurt it. Can't we put some medicine on it? Can't we? Her eyes reflected the truth, but she quickly entered the kitchen and returned with the can of salve she kept there. She rubbed a small glob on the bird's bloody breast, then stepped back and looked at her son whose own chest was bloody where he cradled the bird.

She had to fight back tears when she told him the bird was doomed. Garth held the weakly protesting robin close to his breast as though he was still a baby holding his old teddy bear. No, he said, it's not true, I'll take it to Doc Robinson's drugstore. Doc'll know what to do. He turned to dash with his precious handful of life when he felt it give a strange flutter and heard what, for the rest of his days, he would remember as a groan. Looking down, he saw the small head shudder, then flop limply to one side; one glowing eye suddenly dimmed and became a dull lead BB.

Oh, he cried, oh no, and his mother wanted to hold and comfort him, but he leapt away, sprinting nowhere as fast as he could, wild with the inchoate notion he could somehow flee. But run as he might, and weep, the robin remained dead.

Before Dishonor

So anyways, I's just settin there a-sippin on a bottle of Bud
and trying to score a few points with this cute little waitress,
see, when this ol boy slipped onto the stool next to me. You
must be a tough hombre, he sneered at me, his voice soundin
like he's a-gonna laugh. He reached out and touched my
forearm right where that tattoo says Death Before Dishonor,
and I knowed I was into it. Again. Yessir, says he, you must
be real bad news.

This ol boy he figured he's mighty rough, see, and he's
gonna make me squirm some, then whup me. Well I been
through that little number before, I'll tell you, more than
any once. Yessir, said this ol boy real loud, there must be
one beat up Okie somewhere in the world—he looked
around to make sure everybody at the bar's a-listenin—cause
every Okie I ever knew claimed he never lost a fight. Hell,
they're all such chickenshits, they wouldn't fight no one but
each other, so they all must be whuppin the same poor slob.

Then he laughed, He-he-he, and that's when I decor-
ated his dentures with my beer bottle, while he's still laughin
and feelin big. I knocked him right off his stool onto the
floor, then I did me a little turkey-in-the-straw on his chest.
I never stuck around that joint for no congratulations; I got
the hell out and never went back.

You know, there's things a kid does just haunts a man,
specially if the kid and the man are the same guy. I mean
that fight's the kinda stuff happens to me all the time since—
when was it, fifteen year ago now—I got that damned tattoo

in the first place. Me and this ol boy named Bucky James we was just out of boot camp down by San Diego, see, so we ended up with these two Mexican gals at a tattoo parlor in Tijuana. Well Bucky he got a devil dog on his calf. Me, I just had to have one of them Death Before Dishonor jobs, all done up in fancy writin, red and blue, right on my forearm where nobody could miss it, and not many as have.

The scab hadn't hardly peeled off before every ol boy in the barracks was teasin me. Tough guy, huh! some feller'd say, then Wham! we'd be hot after it. Oh, I had me a few beefs alright.

The worst one come up in Modesto when I's home on leave. This ol boy named Travis King him and me hit a Fats Domino dance, see. We'd been drinkin Thunderbird, snot-flingin drunk when we drove over from Patterson, Travis behind the wheel. We buzzed through them fields and orchards at one-twenty-per, each of us holdin a short dog of T-bird between our legs—our second bottles—listenin to ol Lefty Frizzell on the radio, us not talkin much. Every once and awhile ol Travis he'd look over at me and grin and kindly yodel: Damn right I'm drunk! Then he'd pull the car back onto the road and fishtail for a quarter mile, nearly jammin a cotton truck one time, runnin a station wagon off the road another time, and scarin piss out of a Mexican irrigator one other time. But ol Travis he could drive; we had us one hell of a ride, but we got to the dance anyways.

But he sure as hell couldn't fight a lick, Travis. We no sooner got in the dance hall and seen all them lovely young things just a-twistin and a-twirlin, me hornier than a prairie preacher, when Travis he commenced arguing with a great big ol Wop boy he knowed from high school. Well things got real hot between em directly, so the next thing I knew we was all marchin out to the parkin lot so Travis and this ol boy could settle things.

Maybe the fresh air sobered him, but soon as we hit the pavement, ol Travis crawfished. And that just made the other guy twice as brave; he really called Travis down. All the other guys commenced sayin Travis was chickenshit, and the big guy slapped him right across the face. I figured Travis'd sock the guy, but no, he pointed over at me and

said real loud: By God, you couldn't do that to ol Jerrall!
He's a Marine. Show him your tattoo, Jerrall!

Well, Travis he was wrong. That big ol boy could do
it to me, so I socked him, then he commenced to stomp
livin shit out of me. I was just welts on top of bruises when
it all ended. Travis he helped me back to the car, then drove
me home. He felt so bad about things he had to drink what
was left of my wine. He's goddamned lucky I was so beat-
up, cause I sure as hell would have give him a whuppin if
I could have stood up.

Right after the truckin company transferred me to
McFarland last year I felt pretty low for awhile. I never
knew no one down here. But after while I found this little
beer bar in Delano where a lot of other boys from the truck
company and the sheds hung out, and I got to know lots
of em.

There was this cute little gal named Billie Bea who

worked there, and I taken a shine to her right off. She was
cute as a bug's ear, with the bounciest little rear end you
ever seen. I just yearned to get me some of that.

Billie Bea she never got real friendly with any of the
boys who hung out at the beer bar. I asked around and
nobody claimed he'd got her; only a couple'd even dated
her. She's a church-goer, this one ol boy told me, sanctified
I think. That didn't sound right cause I couldn't figure no
sanctified woman servin beer. Then this guy says the only
thing turns Billie Bea on is roller derby.

Well, I can tell you that ol boy was dead right about
roller derby. I'd noticed the way Billie Bea'd shut everybody
at the bar up whenever them goofy skaters come on the
television set. If she was hot for roller derby, I figured I'd
lay me a scheme. I've had me some experience nailin sanctified sisters when they're all lathered up right after meetin,
so I didn't figure this could be too different.

Now I didn't give a rat's ass for roller derby, never
did. I figured it's a fake. Wrestling, that's my sport. Ol
Argentina Rocca is the greatest athlete that ever was, by
God. Argentina he could jump seven foot; he knocked ol
Rocky Maricano cold one time just messin around; he run
four minute miles every mornin to build his wind. Hell, he
killed lots of guys in the ring, but the press they hushed it
up. Roller derby, it's a knowed fact that it's fake. Them
guys're half queer anyways.

But there wasn't a hell of a lot I wouldn't do to nail
Billie Bea, so I bought me some roller derby magazines and
commenced studyin up in em. Next time I was in the joint
where she worked and I seen her leanin on the bar not talkin
to nobody as usual, I kind of casual announced: Them
Bombers sure been doin good since ol Chico Quirana
joined up.

Billie Bea she kind of blinked and looked at me. Come
again, she said. So I come again. Right away she commenced jabberin: They sure have, she said, but I believe
Ben Benson's the real star. Now he's a jammer! But them
Outlaws could whup em if they'd get rid of all the niggers
on the team. That's all that holds em down, niggers.

Well, anyways, the ice was busted and pretty soon I

had me a date to take her down to Bakersfield for the
monthly roller derby at the fairgrounds.

     When I picked up Billie Bea that evenin she liked to
took my breath away. Now she's always a looker, see, but
that evenin she was like a new wildflower, her hair all piled
on top of her head in a tower of curls, and wearin one of the
miniest skirts I ever seen with these slick white boots. Boy
howdy! I like to nailed her right there. I couldn't hardly
breathe, and I had trouble just walkin out to the car with
her, that bottom of her's a-twitchin like two wildcats in a
gunny sack.
     We ate dinner at this little Mexican restaurant next to
the fairgrounds, Billie Bea purrin and me hornier'n a boar
mouse. After dinner we drank us a couple beers, then walked
to the big hall where the derby was held. In line waitin for
tickets, Billie Bea she stood real close, kinda rubbin on me.
     The hall was a huge, cement-floored stock barn that
smelled a little like last year's manure. Temporary bleachers
was set up around a portable wooden track, and right next
to the track was metal foldin chairs; I'd bought us tickets
for them chairs right next to the track.
     I could tell Billie Bea's blood was risin soon as we
come into the building and heard the skaters warmin up.
We set down and I bought us a couple more beers; Billie
Bea she commenced hollerin at the Outlaws, pointin at
different niggers on the Outlaw team, tellin me how stupid
and chickenshit they was.
     Just then this big ol buck in a Outlaw uniform he skated
right up to where we sat and stopped. He kinda glanced at
me, then turned to Billie Bea and said: What's happenin,
baby? Billie Bea she spit somethin back at him, but he just
laughed and off he rolled. After that Billie Bea she stewed
for a while.
     People kept movin in, settin all around us, all kinds of
folks. Directly in back of where we sat, a little boy in a
miniature derby uniform chawed uncooked spaghetti he
dipped into an open jar of peanut butter held between his
legs. He looked at me like he figured I was gonna snitch
some of it, so I grinned at him. He grinned back. It looks

like shit but it ain't, he said, and his momma cuffed him up
alongside his head.

I ordered me and Billie Bea each another beer from the
guy that sold in the crowd, and Billie Bea she finally said
to me: You whup that nigger for me, and you won't be
sorry. I started to answer her, but she reached over and
touched my arm. Soon as I seen that tattoo, she told me, I
knew you'd whup one for me. Then she run the point of her
tongue over her lips and I had to cross my legs. Sure, I kinda

croaked. It seemed like a safe thing to say, cause that buck
was on the track and I was drinkin beer in the foldin chairs.
I never give it a thought.

The gals commenced skatin, buzzin and whirrin around
the track so fast you couldn't see em clear till they was on
the other side. All different kinds of gals: fat, skinny, blonde,
all different kind, even coloreds. They could surely skate,
and rough too, a-punchin and jabbin each other and there's
a couple of nigger gals on the Outlaws who skated real
dirty. Billie Bea she told me their names, but I forget.

When the fellers come on the track, things got really
wild, fightin all over and kickin and cussin. There was this
big ol country boy named Ben Benson skatin for the
Bombers he was just slammin the back door on Outlaw
jammers. Next thing I knew, three Outlaws broke away
from the pack, knocked the Bombers flat who was after em,
then closed on the country boy. Now Benson he's a rough
cob, so he just kinda planted hisself right in their way, and
I could see them Outlaws didn't want to tangle with him.
They kinda slowed down and had a huddle, then on they
come, one big buck in front like he was gonna try to sneak
through, and the other two laggin along behind like they
was ascared.

Just when the buck caught up to Benson, and country
boy Ben moved over to knock him flat, them other two Outlaw jammers they roared up from behind and never made
no effort to get by. Naw, they jumped on Benson and took
him down, and that buck nigger he commenced kickin him.
Well pretty soon both teams was hot after it, fellas and gals.
And everyone from the stands they run up next to the track
and screamed. A couple beefs broke out right in the crowd.

I noticed how that big buck nigger was just kinda layin
on Ben Benson not more'n ten feet from where I stood. It
almost looked like they was laughin together, but I knowed
it was rage on their faces. Billie Bea she seen em too, and
she said to me: Get that nigger now, honey. Well, by God,
I was just in the mood to whup me a nigger by that time,
so I vaulted right over the railin and headed for the bastard.
He never seen me coming, and I wound up one hell of a
Sunday punch.

That's about all I recollect, till I looked up into the lights and seen this dark thing over me, and felt kind of a weight on my chest. I finally focused on eyes and a mouth: it was a face, by God, a nigger face right over mine. It was a nigger gal's face! She spit right on me and said: You crazy mofuckah! I started to kick her ass, then all of a sudden I was chokin; some bastard'd pinned my neck to the track with his skate and out of the corner of my eye I seen Ben Benson was steppin on me. Right next to him stood that buck.

Whenever they let me up I's weaker'n a popcorn fart, and I seen I had blood all over me. My lips were swole; one eye and my nose just ached. Get you ass outa here, that nigger gal she screamed, and all them other skaters menaced me. I climbed back through the railin, and damned if folks in the crowd didn't commence tryin to sock me. Thank God a couple deputies was right there to walk me out to my car. Billie Bea she wasn't nowhere to be seen.

Once I got to my car I just set there in back of the steerin wheel, my face feelin full of icey spots, new sore places checkin in from all over my body. I set there tryin to make sense of things. Then I noticed that goofy tattoo on my own forearm like I never seen it before, it kinda glowin in a bright slash of light comin through the car window from a street lamp: Death Before Dishonor. You know, she's a rough ol life, but you got to take 'er like she comes. I noticed that tattoo and commenced chucklin; I couldn't help myself. Then I giggled, then laughed, then I just roared. Death Before Dishonor, and me laying on that track with a little nigger gal straddlin me spittin in my face. Boy howdy!

Well at least I ain't been killed yet.

Wild Goose:
Memories of a Valley Summer

Like a shimmering, solitary tombstone, the shed looms from barren winter fields before me as I drive down the valley toward home. Growing on the horizon, swelling till I see clearly the track, the old wooden deck, and the ice house in back, all empty. The memory smell of grapes sweeps me as I buzz past, as though the gnarled fruitless vines staked carefully over the fields have instantly burgeoned; it's really the accumulated juice of a billion trodden grapes returning as odor from the shed's floors and walls. I'm past the building in a sliced instant, but the thawing aroma of grapes stays with me, intoxicates me.

Everything had smelled ripe that hot summer when, fifteen-years-old, I worked at Corso and Sons' Grape Packing Shed. The empty boxcars reeked of creosote; girls were musky and exciting; grapes smelled of earth and life. In the harsh sunlight of a San Joaquin Valley summer, everything leaped at you, everything entered you. The big building swarmed with life in its season, making up with intensity what it lacked in duration, for it lived only two months a year.

I'd labored during preceding summers in the fields— picking grapes and potatoes, thinning sugar beets, chopping cotton—so the chance to work at a shed was too good to refuse. I started as a trucker, transporting with a hand-truck stack after stack of cartons loaded with table grapes, pushing them from the place where other workers stacked the cartons next to a conveyor belt, across the wooden deck built around the shed, over a metal ramp and into a boxcar standing on the company's siding. Inside the cars the men called loaders quickly, yet carefully, positioned the cartons, then nailed them secure with wooden slats.

The deck around the building was the same height as the boxcar's floors; truckers had only to ease their heavily loaded vehicles over a wide metal ramp bridging the three feet between deck and car. Speed was essential to efficient loading, so ramps were not nailed to either the deck or the car's floor, enabling a crew to move them from a freshly loaded boxcar to an empty in a moment, shifting the ramp so fast they didn't fall behind the conveyer belts' production of newly packed cartons. But the steady traffic of hand trucks jostled the loose ramp, gradually changing its position; unless returned to its original place, it might fall— trucker and all—onto the tracks below. Experienced hands kept their ramp properly positioned without thought, jarring it back into place with their empty truck as they returned to the belt for another load. Novices sometimes forgot.

On my second day at work I was the only trucker carrying crates from a particularly slow conveyer. Shortly after lunch, my belly full, I drowsily pushed my loaded truck onto a ramp, only to find with sudden clarity the ramp gone; I felt myself pulled—sucked almost—into the void by the heavy truck, then a quick jolt, then nothing. I heard laughter, but could not see it and, looking down, saw above me the narrow slash of sky between deck and car; my head ached. Throwing splintered wood and grape slush from me, I slowly unwound upward like a fakir's rope. On the deck, Chico, the crew pusher, stood, hands on his thin hips, glaring at me. "You O.K.?" I wasn't sure, but I replied, "Yes sir." "Good. Clean up yer mess. Ever' new boy gits one a them wrecks give him. Do it again and yer canned," he said, whirling away and disappearing on his last word. I didn't do it again.

Most of us who worked at the shed were Okies, though there was a sprinkling of Negroes and Mexicans and Filipinos. And most Okies at the shed were second-generation kids like me, whose parents had struggled into California from the Midwest or Southwest during dust bowl days.

My daddy had come out from West Texas in the mid-thirties with, he told me, seventeen cents in his pocket when he blew into Bakersfield. After several years of bare survival working the crops in the central valley, he'd been hired by an oil company. We'd been relatively secure throughout my life; I was never really hungry and I didn't even have to work during the school year. My uncle was a field foreman on a big potato farm, and he'd always found a job for me in the summer. Few of my friends were so lucky. Many had quit school and a few my age were already married.

We truckers ate our lunches on the wooden deck next to the ice house. The syrupy heat of the valley was somewhat less oppressive next to the ice, though the flow of hot talk was almost as bad as open sunlight. Stories burst bomb-like from young men, each story more grand than the one preceding. "Pore ol' Mary King," one cable-like kid said solemnly, mentioning the name of a particularly pretty girl who worked grading grapes on the conveyer line inside the shed, "she shore does like it. Me and Bucky both got her after work the other day." I was astounded, for I'd often admired Mary King from afar.

"That ain't nothin'," Bubba Hulke responded quickly. "I can get her any time I want. Hell, we even go to the same church."

"Why," preened Harley Pratt, who was the only other young guy from my neighborhood working for Corso's, "she calls me up all the time begging for it!"

"Shit!" I said, after searching for just the right word.

Before Harley could erupt into curses, Bubba Hulke, who was older and larger than either of us, closed the discussion of Mary King: "Pore girl's bound to die in childbirth," he pronounced. It seemed reasonable. For days afterwards I looked at the beautiful Mary King, but was unable to detect any of the tell-tale signs of a whore: large breasts, pimples, bad teeth, thick ankles.

Harley and I had never been really close friends, though we'd been in the class together from the first grade. His older brother, Redford, was a stud, always talking about guys he'd whupped and girl's he'd got. He even claimed to be an experienced drinker—"That sloe gin; now that's a real drank," he'd condescended to tell me once. Working together that summer, I started eating with Harley and Redford and other older guys Redford's age. I like to hear them talk about fighting, and the Marine Corps, and Tijuana bibles.

One long, slow afternoon, when government inspectors had stopped the conveyor belts because the grapes contained insufficient sugar, we lazed in the shade, half angry because we weren't paid when the belts stopped and knowing if we took off we'd be canned. Redford began kidding Harley about a fight he'd lost recently to a scrawny little Mexican kid about half his size. Harley took the bait, reddening and sputtering as Bubba, who was a cousin of the Pratts, joined the game. Finally, in a burst of frustrated rage, Harley volunteered to whip me. The older boys sanctioned the bout and in a moment I was rolling around jabbing and gouging at Harley, biting his cheek and finally pinning him like a dead insect. As far as I was concerned the fight was over, then Redford kicked me, missing my head, landing solidly on my shoulder.

I managed to stand before he attacked again and,

luckily, I arose with my back to the shed's wall. Redford stood in front of me, a sick grin on his face: "You little son-of-a-bitch," he spat, "I'm a-gonna teach you to bite my brother." He feinted clumsily and charged, head down, both arms swinging wildly, directly at me. I followed my daddy's teaching and watched him until he was almost on me, then threw one straight punch at his exposed head. To my surprise his knees buckled and he sagged shallow-eyed. I shuffled toward him and started another punch but Bubba slipped behind me and sundayed me to sleep.

After having my face patched that afternoon at a doctor's office in Delano, I was driven back to work by Eugene Corso, the youngest son of Anton Corso who owned the shed and the vast fields surrounding it. Eugene, bronze and thick-necked, played football at U.C.L.A. and his grid exploits were legend in local high school circles. He iced boxcars and helped his old man manage the shed during the summer.

"You did pretty good against those Pratts," Eugene told me. "I think you could licked 'em all one at a time."

I glowed with pride.

"Yeah," he went on, "I took care of old Redford myself the first summer he worked for us. You just let me know if they get after you."

Eugene sort of adopted me after that, letting me eat lunch with his circle of friends; two of the guys were college football players like Eugene, Washington Phillips and Johnny Dominguez, and the other two were loaders, Roger and Dick Renfro. The Renfros were cousins, both tall, stringy men, old guys maybe thirty or thirty-five. The football players were weight-lifters, full of energy, always jumping around and raising hell, while Roger and Dick seemed lazy and slow, with concave chests and buzzard necks. But nobody took liberties with them I noticed soon enough. Sometimes Chico, the pusher, joined us.

We usually ate in the ice shack, for as chief ice man Eugene ruled that part of the shed. Other workers would sit, as I had before my fateful fight with the Pratts, on the shaded deck outside the shack and lean against the building's cool walls, but only Eugene's friends got inside.

Johnny Dominguez brought homemade burritos for lunch every single day. I'd never tasted one, and they looked so tempting that I asked him one day to trade me for my deviled-meat sandwich and he agreed. Inside the burrito were the beans I expected, but different, all squashed with little hot peppers that tingled more than burned, and meat and cheese; it was the dangest thing I'd ever eaten. "God, that's good," I said.

"Your sandwich would gag a maggot, hey" Johnny answered, the other men chuckling. "Who ever heard of ketchup and mustard on deviled meat?"

"That's a okie burrito," Wash countered, laughing at the sour-faced Johnny.

"Gawwd damn. It's no wonder you Okies are so skinny, hey, eatin' this shit." Johnny shook his head in mock despair, but he kept eating.

Roger Renfro, who seemed to speak like a man just awakened from deep sleep, grinned at Johnny. "Hell," he said, "we keep in shape just a-whuppin' Mescans." Everyone broke up. The Renfros and Johnny nibbled at dried red peppers while they ate lunch, though neither Wash nor Eugene touched them. Dick Renfro held a pepper toward me: "You orta try one a these, by God. It'll put some lead in yer pencil." He turned to Johnny: "Give the kid one a them peppers, Juano." Wash and Eugene giggled.

"I don't think I need one a them," I said, wary.

"Don't be a pussy," chided Wash.

"You eat one then."

"Right after you," he said.

I was beginning to think my ice shack lunches were over as they all looked at me, quieting a bit. "Take it," ordered Johnny softly. I took it.

"You ain't got hair on yer ass if you don't eat it at one gulp," Dick said, gulping one himself to show what he meant.

Eugene was looking at me hard, saying nothing, and I knew I had to. I ate it and suddenly my mouth was full of bee stings. Everyone was watching me intently, as, eyes watering, I tried to chew; my throat began to burn and my mouth passed beyond pain to a dull ice heat, then my throat caught the full fury and I could stand it no longer. As much as I hated to give them an inch, I leaped up and ran for the water faucet while they collapsed in laughter.

For a while after the pepper was only a stinging memory in my mouth and throat, and a cube of discomfort in my belly, I stood apart from them near the water, boiling at them for having laughed at me. It was about time to go back to work, and they were still talking about me and carrying on. I must have looked pretty silly. They got up and headed back toward their jobs and I looked away only to feel a nudge in my ribs. It was Roger.

"Here's yer dinner bucket," he said sleepily. "Take you a bite a this." He handed me his plug of chewing tobacco. "It'll take the hot away." I nodded, my throat was still too seared to speak. "You might make a hand yet," he said. Next day we all ate together like nothing had happened.

Roger and Dick had this thing about them: they were goosey; no, they were super-goosey. You could sneak up behind one of them and lightly jab him anywhere, saying a word as you did it, and he'd leap forward wildly, screeching the word you'd said. When Eugene told me about it I didn't

believe him. Who would? So he demonstrated.

The two loaders had just joined us for lunch that day, and Eugene sort of sidled behind Roger and dug a finger into his ribs, saying: "Bullshit!" Roger exploded into the air like a man kicking a football, leg thrusting out while his arms swung wide and he wailed in a high voice "Ohhhhhh bullshit!"

"My heart goes where the wild goose goes..." Eugene chanted as Roger jerked spasmodically across the room like a toy running down, the contents of his lunch pail spread over the floor. Everyone except Dick was laughing, but my laughter was more nervous than amused; I'd never seen anything like that before and it made me uncomfortable; it just didn't seem right for a man to jerk and wail.

When Roger angrily grabbed Eugene and threw him to the floor I was glad. "I'll show you a fuckin' wild goose," he spat, his left hand on the larger man's throat, his right fist cocked as he sat astride Eugene's broad chest. "Try this little goose for size."

"Don't," said Eugene, and to my amazement, Roger didn't. He sat there on Eugene's chest, glaring, his right hand cocked. "God damnit, Eugene, I told you about that stuff. I could of killed someone if I'd of had my hatchet in my hand, or even my dinner bucket. Ain't you ever gonna grow-up?" Eugene said nothing and Roger just sat there for a long time. A lot of guys were looking in the shed's door to see the fight, but nothing happened. Dick and Wash and Johnny just sat there watching, and pretty soon Roger stood and deliberately picked up Eugene's lunch. "You eat mine," he said to Eugene, "you fucked it up." Eugene ate what was left of Roger's lunch without complaint, winking at me once. Roger and Dick seemed to eat very fast and they left us long before it was time to work again.

"Man, he something!" Wash said as soon as they left. "I heard about that but, man, I never saw anything like it before. He something else."

Near the end of the summer I became a loader. Eugene talked his old man into trying me as a substitute for one of the old-timers who couldn't seem to stay sober long enough

to work. I was much younger—though not much smaller—
than any others, so Chico assigned me to Dick Renfro.
"This little old boy wants to be a loader," Chico told him.
"See if he can cut 'er, Dick."

Once you develop the rhythm, the feel, for loading
grape cartons it's not bad work. It's cool in the boxcars and
the steady tempo helps time pass quickly. You've got to
move fast yet gently. The difficult part is nailing slats across
each tier of cartons with swift, sure strokes driving the short
nails only into the thick end pieces of cartons, hitting hard
enough to penetrate with a single tap, yet lightly enough
not to splinter the cartons.

All loaders carried hammer-head hatchets for nailing
slats; it was their badge. When a man walked through the
shed with a hatchet tucked in his belt, everyone knew he
was a loader. When a kid walked through with a hatchet,
all the girls knew he was something special. I wore my
hatchet prominently, and managed to walk through the shed
a dozen times during those first days, especially when the
conveyer belts were all shut down and the young girls, most
of them riper than the grapes, weren't too busy to notice me.

Dick was a good teacher, seldom wasting his breath to
lecture me; instead he showed me how it was done and
worked alongside me. When lulls occurred, I'd comb my
hair and stroll, hatchet prominently displayed, levis droop-
ing, through the shed, but Dick took to teasing me; "Looky
there," he'd say to Roger or Chico or anyone within earshot,
"hair all slicked down like a preacher after meetin'. Fixin'
to get him some nooky. Probably gonna take up a collection,
too." So I stopped parading my wares, however meagre,
and began to sit in the boxcar during free time telling stories
with the Renfros and Chico and the rest.

One day Dick and Chico jumped me during a break in
work. They were going to pants me and throw me out of the
boxcar bare-assed. Well, old Chico got to laughing so hard
he soon let me go, and Dick and I scuffled around the car,
both laughing. Most of us were great fans of T.V. wrestling
and Dick was no exception; in the midst of our energetic
mock-combat, he kept warning me about the holds he was
about to apply: "Look out for the abdominal stretch....Here

comes my atomic drop!"

We did little more than clutch and hug one another. Eventually Dick slithered one of his wirey arms around my neck and bent me nearly to the floor, saying: "By God now you'll get my Japanese sleep hold." At that moment my half-hearted thrashing to escape jammed the handle of my hatchet into Dick's ribs. I sprawled to the floor before I realized what had happened: Dick, his right leg swinging a violent arc, bounced across the boxcar's floor. "Ohhhhhh sleep hold!" he cried, his arms flailing wildly. I didn't even have time to get scared.

Chico collapsed in tearful laughter before Dick's head even stopped bobbing. Dick glared for a dark moment at me, then began laughing too. "By God," Chico managed to gasp, "he give you the Canadian goose hold." And we all laughed ourselves silly until the loaders at the shed had come to our car to see what was happening.

Government inspectors worked at the shed, checking to make certain the sugar content of the fruit was above the established minimum for the table grapes. The inspectors' edicts often shut us down, as they found produce from one particular field lacking, and we waited for a new batch to come in from the pickers. The boss was restive when work stopped, and lots of times I saw bottles of liquor being loaded into an inspector's auto. Most of the older inspectors, Eugene told me, had arrived at mutually beneficial under-standings with his father. But late that season a red-hot team of young inspectors took over at the shed and we seemed to be stopped more often than not. Old Anton Corso stalked around the place red-faced, his two-dollar cigar puffing like the fuse on an anarchist's bomb.

We'd been shut down for most of one long August afternoon, and everyone was restless; workers clustered around the building talking, playing cards, eating grapes. A gang of us lolled in Roger's boxcar telling stories and chewing tobacco. Johnny was midway through a gang fight with some guys from *la loma*, embellishing the tale with just enough Spanish to keep us wondering, when I noticed

Eugene kind of sneaking over behind Roger and winking at me.

Johnny finished his epic, and Roger started telling us about a fabulous character named Fat Gray who once worked at the shed. He could drive nails by throwing his hatchet from across the boxcar, and he threw it funny— Roger took his hatchet from his belt to show us how. Eugene was directly behind him now, and no one but me seemed to notice him standing there with the beginning of a smirk on his face. I knew I had to warn Roger. An indistinct, overwhelming fear blossomed in me, yet I did nothing. Absolutely nothing.

Shouting "Wild goose!" Eugene poked Roger in the back and, with sudden certainty, Roger's arms flew out and behind like a swimmer's, planting the hatchet in Eugene's grinning face, splitting his nose and seeming to crack his head—opening pale for a frozen instant, then gushing bright. Roger had been half-squatting when he was poked, and he hunched violently across the floor like a heat-crazed dog. "Ohhhhhh wild goose!" he called, halting against the far wall with bounces and jerks. He swirled angrily around, only to see Eugene sitting against the other wall with thick hands fluttering to his melon-masked face, the hatchet still planted where his nose had been.

"Oh sweet Jesus, Eugene," Roger said. "Oh sweet lovin' Jesus." Then he went over and took care of him till the ambulance arrived.

Eugene didn't die. They rushed him to a Bakersfield hospital and saved his life. He never played football again, though, and even the best plastic surgeons couldn't make him look quite the same.

Roger and Dick disappeared. They were canned and black-balled, Chico told me. "We'll never see 'em 'round here no more, not if old man Corso gets his way." I never have seen them since that day, and I didn't work in the shed again after that summer. I liked the money and I liked being a loader, but I knew that sooner or later talk would always get back to Roger and Dick and Eugene and I just didn't want to hear it. "She's a tough one," Chico said, " 'cause, it's really nobody's fault. Gene didn't wanta hurt them boys

and Roger didn't wanta hurt him. Thangs just happened."
But I don't know. I just don't know.

I've seen the big, box-like building a hundred times or
more since it all happened, but I've never even stopped to
look the place over again. I never will.

80

Ace Low

Whenever I seen old Ace Thomas sashay up Chester Avenue, I'd damn near laugh. I mean Ace, he's a little bitty guy and old, maybe forty or fifty, and all scarred-up with a crooked nose and thick eyebrows and knotted knuckles; if you didn't know him you'd swear he was half on his ass. He always dressed like it was still the Depression: tired brown and white oxfords with white sox, and these here seersucker shirts you could see through, and a beat-up old ten-gallon. He looked about like he just carried a bindle in from Highway 99.

Sometimes you'd find him down by the bus stop talkin to old-timers about back home, Ace squattin on his heels just like my granddaddy, suckin on a quid of Mail Pouch and rollin a toothpick around his mouth. And he liked to set on the bench over by the library too, his legs crossed funny, right next to each other, not ankle-to-knee. He was always talkin to the old guys, always lookin sad, like he didn't belong in California at all and wasn't gonna give California a inch. He was about as down home as a guy could be.

The funny thing is that Ace he was married and had him a nice house over on Linda Vista. He had him three boys, too—one just my age—and he sent them boys through college ever one. He owned a big 56 Cadillac car then that his wife drove mostly, and he owned him Ace's Place.

Before they made it legal, Ace had him a card room in back of his little beer bar down in Riverview. It wasn't hid or nothin. Hell, you could see right into it from the shuffleboard. Folks said he paid off the sheriff. Anyways, it was just this old storage room converted to hold a poker table, but it stayed purty crowded.

I heard Ace made his living from cards, and that the beer and shufflboad and pool table didn't do more than pay rent. I can't say for sure about that, but I'll tell you old Ace was damn serious about cards. He just didn't fart around where cards was concerned. Usual, he didn't even go down to his place till the middle of the afternoon when he could raise a game. He just let this here fat gal, Olive, open up and run things most of the day.

Olive she was nice. She let us young bucks hang around and play pool and shuffleboard, but she wouldn't sell us no beer. Old Ace he put up with us most of the time, long as we didn't bother the cash customers, but he wouldn't take no shit off any of us guys, like the time Merle Duncan went after the nigger man.

Merle he was the roughest old boy in high school, no question about it: he could really fight. Not that he was mean, but there was times when it seemed like he couldn't help hisself. And, of course, back in them days wasn't no niggers lived in Oildale or Riverview; folks used to say any nigger in Oildale after dark was dead.

Anyways, it was a summer mornin, hotter than a bygosh, and I didn't drive nothin better than a 40 Chevy. Us guys was nursing soda pops and playin free games of shuffleboard. Olive's husband he'd hurt hisself out on a rig, and she had to stay home to nurse him, so Ace he was workin behind the bar, playing Bob Wills' songs for us on the jukebox and we was teasin him about how he ought to get some good stuff on it like the Platters or Nat "King" Cole. Ace just laughed. All of a sudden, in the front door walks this sad-lookin nigger man and his little boy. We was shocked; nobody said nothin for a minute. This nigger man he took his hat off and held it and he asked Ace: "Mister, is they some little job of work my boy here and me could do for you? Anything at all?" Ace didn't answer right off, he just rolled that toothpick around his mouth like he was studyin up on what the man asked.

The big propeller fan on the ceiling turned for half-a-

minute, then Merle he couldn't resist. I seen him kindly
puffin up like he always did before a fight. He growled:
"Niggers ain't allowed in here!" His fists were doubled up,
his neck swole, and he looked about ready to jump the black
guy.

"Out!" It was Ace, and the nigger man he turned to
leave, his hand on his little boy's shoulder. "Not you," Ace
said. "Him!" He was lookin at Merle.

"Wait a fuckin minute!" Merle hollered real loud.

Ace kept lookin right at him: "This man come in here
lookin for work. He never hurt nobody. You lazy bastard,
you ain't got nothin to say to him. Out!"

I don't know if Merle was fixin to whup Ace or the
nigger, cause he never got to either one of em. He just
moved toward the front; old Ace come over the bar with
this here sawed-off pool cue he kept, and Whap! He caught
Merle right on the shoulder, then he hit him twice more on
the rear while he's on the floor. "Out!" he said.

Merle was cryin, "My daddy's a-gonna kick your ass,"
as he staggered out. Ace never even answered. But Merle's
daddy never bothered Ace, and Ace he put the nigger man
and his boy to work washin windows.

Us guys never went back to Ace's for a long time after
that, but there wasn't a hell of a lot to do in Oildale back
then, or now either. After a month of hangin around Stand-
ard School, we kindly mozied back to Ace's, and he never
said nothin, not even to Merle. My granddaddy told me:
"Hell, that little setee warn't even a pimple on Ace's butt,"
and I spose he was right. But when that big-time badass
from West Texas come to town, by God, that was a boil!

I recollect it good, cause it was my first year in the
oilfields right after I quit high school and I was feelin flat
rich. I had me a brand new 58 Studebaker—"Stud Wacker"
I called it—and my shit didn't stink. All the guys treated me
mighty special that year. I'd hit old Ace's right after work
and hang around there till about seven or eight ever evenin,
just playin pool or listenin to Lefty Frizzell on the juke box,
or maybe watchin the Cousin Herb T.V. show.

But one night—not really night since it was still light
and hot—in strutted this badass and two of his boys. The

West Texan he was a driller on a wildcat rig workin out by Buttonwillow, and he'd heard of the game Ace run. So he blew into Ace's with two roughnecks from his crew just as the afternoon crowd was leaving. As luck would have it, there wasn't a game yet that night, so Ace he was behind the bar with Olive.

"Where's the big shot card player?" This West Texan he demanded.

Ace never batted a eye. "What'll she be?" he asked real friendly.

Me, I decided I'd stick around a while longer.

"I'm Clyde Milsap from Lubbock," this big driller announced, "and I got me twenty-five hundred bucks cash money in my pocket. I heard there's a old boy hangs out here ain't afraid to play a little cards. Ain't you got no Ernest Tubbs on that juke box?"

Ace drew all three of them boys brews. "What kinda stakes you figger on playin?"

"Ten bucks minimum. No limit," grunted Milsap, and I could see he'd caught on to who Ace was.

"Sounds reasonable," Ace said. "You boys bring your beers in back." He led them into the card room, then turned on the light. Two old-timers, this guy called Lucky, and another guy named Floyd, they joined the table. Me, I just stood by the door and watched while Milsap took off his jacket, and I seen the two biggest arms in the world; his tattoos just rippled.

"Low ball?" Ace asked.

"Name your fate," said Milsap.

Well, low ball was Ace's game. Period. It was Ace's. But old Milsap didn't look like nothin wasn't his game. And when the cards started, it seemed that a-way too. He took the first two hands when Ace threw his in without callin. Them other guys was just fillin chairs. They didn't do shit otherwise. Wasn't more than a hundred hit the table them hands anyhow.

Third hand, though, the poker commenced. Ace must have drew low, cause he only asked for one card, then smiled. Milsap he needed three, the Ace quick pushed a crisp hundred-dollar-bill out, and the other four boys threw their cards in. Milsap seen him and called with a extra fifty. Ace took him seven-five-four-three-ace low, and both of em was hot after it.

Next hand Ace stood pat, kindly smilin again. Milsap drew three. Ace pushed $250.00 out onto the table and ever one but Milsap folded. The big West Texan he licked his lips and seen Ace. Ace picked up another hundred like he was fixin to toss it into the pot, and Milsap crawfished. I was standing behind Ace, and I'll tell you, he didn't have no hand a-tall.

I come back about midnight after a date, and they's still at the table. Floyd was long gone, and Lucky he was suckin wind with his ass. I believe old Milsap was helpin his two pals out and maybe in the long run that's what whupped him. Cause about two A.M. he was stoney broke. Didn't have a pot to pee in or a window to throw her out of. And he was sore.

"You been cheatin you little prick!" he menaced. His

two boys both jumped up and so did he. "You cheatin son-
of-a-bitch!" he went on, red-faced and twitchin them tattoos
on his arms. Them other two looked about ready to lynch
old Ace.

"Nobody has to cheat when they play roustabouts,"
Ace told em. "You boys oughta stick to your own jobs?
Cards is mine. I don't go out to your rig and tell you how to
find oil."

That's when Milsap swung. He threw that big right
fist of his at Ace and I figgered he'd kill him, but old Ace
ducked under easy as you please. "If you boys're fixing to
play rough," he said, reachin under the table, "then I'll
have to."

The three of em really got a kick out of that. "Yeah,"
old Milsap spat, his face as tight as a baby's britches, "we're
fixin to play damn rough." He no sooner'n got that last word
out, than old Ace he stood up and reached across the table
with his big old .44 he'd took from a slot built into the table
where he always sat.

Before Milsap could duck or run, Ace squeezed off a
round right next to that Texan's ear: POW! Them other
two roughnecks was already gone, sparks flying from their
feet they run so fast. Milsap he just kindly stood there
across the table rockin on his heels, his eyes lookin like
Little Orphan Annie's; he figgered he's dead, I believe.

"Get your ass out a here!" Ace told him. He leveled
that big Oklahoma hogleg right at Milsap's gizzard. All of
a sudden, Milsap he reached up and grabbed his head, then
his eyes bugged out and he took off like a fresh-cut calf.

Me, I's standin right by the door, and I swear Milsap
never even looked pissed; he looked happy to be alive. He
never stopped for his 48 Lincoln either, he just kept a-
sprintin and a good thing he did. Ace kindly strolled to the
front door, made sure there wasn't no traffic, then squeezed
off a couple more shots at Milsap's feet, and that big old
Texan, evertime one a them bullets busted up dirt, he just
let her out another notch. Two-thirds of the way down the
block, damned if Milsap didn't pass old Snake Werts, this
drunk that was always around. Well, Snake he kindly blinked
when he seen that big bastard run by him, and he didn't

wait. I guess he figured if there was somethin up the street
mean enough to make a guy big as Milsap run, he didn't
need none of it.

Just as they reached the end of the block, Snake
caught up to Milsap and commenced passin him, then they
hit a street repair project and the two of em lost traction in
the loose gravel. Milsap was tryin to turn the corner and
Snake was in his way. They clawed and crawled one another,
both of em gettin nowheres, when old Ace he squeezed off
another round and busted the gravel up around their feet.
That done her! Milsap liked to paved the road with Snake,
runnin clean out of his suede boots and over Werts, who
was flat by then.

Lucky went and fetched Snake and brought him, and
Milsap's boots too, back to Ace's place. Old Snake he never
missed a chance for a free drink. Soon as he seen it was Ace
that was doin the shootin, he brightened up. "I liked to
caught him fer ya, Ace," he said. "I had him good down by
the corner whenever I slipped." Ace laughed, then told
Snake beer was on the house.

But that wasn't the end of it a-tall. Milsap he let word
get out he was fixin to kill Ace. He wasn't used to bein
humiliated, I reckon, and it must've really burned him.
Grandaddy said: "Me, if I's simple enough to go after Ace,
I sure as hell wouldn't let *him* know about it. He never
lasted this long bein soft." But Milsap spread the word all
over Kern County that he's fixin to plug Ace.

So Ace never waited. He took his big hogleg, climbed into Milsap's Lincoln, and off he sped for Buttonwillow where the Texan's crew was drillin. "I believe I'll return that big gambler's car and boots," was all he said.

Well, we waited all day, and Ace he never come back. Olive she was so worried she forgot herself and sold me and Merle each a draft, and I bought old Snake a couple too. Lucky was there, and he finally told Olive to turn on the radio and see if there'd been a shootin out at Buttonwillow, but we didn't hear a thing. Come supper time, it seemed like half of Oildale was waitin at Ace's, even his oldest boy, Doyle, had showed up and I never had seen him there before. Ace he never let his family near barrooms.

Pretty soon we seen Milsap's 48 Lincoln chuggin down Chester Avenue. Up it pulled and old Ace was behind the wheel. Chee-rist on a crutch did he look beat! He looked like he'd been shot at and missed, and shit at and hit. Ace he just set there in the car kindly suckin his breath, us all around him wantin to know what'd happened.

"Well," Ace finally grunted, "that old boy's on his way back to West Texas. He ain't a-gonna bother us no more."

"Goddamn, Ace," I busted out, "he beat piss outa you. It looks like your nose is busted."

Ace turned his head in my direction. "It might be at that," he conceded, then he showed us his shootin hand and it was all swole and purple; "I believe this hand is busted too, and couple short ribs on the other side. Sure as hell made drivin hard. But Milsap got him a few bruises."

"God, I sure hope so," said old Lucky. "Scoot over partner, and I'll drive you over to Mercy Hospital."

Very slowly, Ace scooted, groanin a little and having to squint his eyes a bit. Then he seen Doyle: "What're you doin down here, son?" he asked kindly sharp.

"I just heard about what was happenin, Daddy, and I was worried."

"I 'preciate that," Ace answered, "but this ain't no place for a boy. Go home and tell Momma I'm okey, but I'll be a little late." When Doyle turned to go, Ace smiled. "He's a good boy," he said. "Got all A's on his last report."

Lucky started the car, and old Ace's eyes caught mine,

then Merle's. "You two orta be back in school where you belong, not hangin around no beer joints, or you'll end up like us, scratchin out a livin all your lives."

I felt embarrassed and didn't answer, but old Merle never had sense, and he started a "Yeah, but..."

Ace never let him finish. "Reach in my pocket on this side," he ordered. "There's a little souvenir there to show you boys how much fun it is to be a barroom hero."

Merle reached in and pulled out one of Milsap's ears.

She's My Rock

Me and some other boys had stole us a case of Lucky from this truck that was deliverin to the Tejon Club, and we was flat frog-eyed whenever we drove into the Mohawk Serv-U-Self on Norris Road. I was a-fillin the tank when old Clyde Mays he come back from the pisser a-gigglin and carryin on; "There's a gal over in yonder van," he said, "that's hot for your body." He pointed toward a U-haul gassin up at the next island.

Well, I believed him. Why shouldn't I? I mean I wasn't half-bad lookin, and besides that, I was drunk, so I wandered over to that van, unbuttonin my shirt and pullin my jeans down a bit so whoever the gal was could see my built. When I got to the van, I looked in the side door and seen these skinny legs bendin over in a big mess of watermelons. I crinkled my eyes up so I'd look like Ferlin Huskey, then I said: "Howdy."

The gal looked-up and Lordy! That's the ugliest gal I ever did see, and a harelip to boot. "Nya wanna buy a waner-melon?" she asked me, and I guess she was smilin, her lip all pulled up into her nose like someone mended it on a foot-pedal sewing machine. That made me laugh, picturing some fat old doctor puttin this here ugly baby up on the machine, then whap-whap-whap! sewin her mouth up while her skinny legs was a-kickin a-round.

"Whan's vunny?" she asked, her eyes turnin sad all of a sudden. Well, ugly or not, I couldn't let Clyde know he'd tricked me; sides, I could always get me a flag to put over her face and screw for old glory. I wasn't gonna crawfish on screwin this little old gal any more than I would on a fight, though I believe I'd rather've fought her; who wants to diddle a harelip gal anyways? "I'm just laughin at you in there with all them watermelons," I told her. "Looks to me like they ain't much room to set."

She smiled again. I think.

"Why don't you come over to my car and we can get comfortable in the back seat." I reached out and touched her hand real gentle, just kind of tickled it the way that drives em nuts, and she stayed bent over them watermelons, her eyes gettin big. That's when I realized she was real young; I wasn't but 17 myself, and I'll bet she wasn't more than 14, but that ugly face surely aged her. Anyways, I don't believe she knew what I wanted.

"Hunh?" she asked.

I stepped closer, then touched her thigh, it all warm and smooth and not harelippy a-tall, and I felt her shudder. I was gettin hot all of a sudden myself, and I started wonderin if I really did have a flag in my car. Her eyes just sparked over that tore-up excuse for a mouth. Lord, she was one ugly girl! Ewe-gly! Double-ugly! Still, them eyes and the way her thigh felt, I just figured tail's tail.

Then damned if somebody didn't sock me right on the shoulder, and I heard Clyde and the guys laugh. I spun around with my fists cocked, and there stood this good-lookin gal maybe 35-, 40-years-old; she just spit at me: "You keep your goddamn hands off Nola Sue or I'll kick your pimply butt clean back to Weedpatch!" She meant it. (You know, drunk as I was, I asked myself: How the hell does she know about me having pimples on my butt?)

Smack! She slapped my face. "Nola Sue," she ordered, "you close them doors. I'll deal with this punk," then damned if she didn't bust a watermelon right on my chest, the juice runnin down into my jeans and all.

What could I do? That lady she had me by the short hairs. I mean I couldn't sock her. Besides, she's meaner than cat shit, and I didn't know for sure if I could whup her; some of them old honky tonk gals is mighty rough. So I just hustled back to my 40 Chevy, tryin to act like I thought it was a big joke, with that watermelon all over me and flies buzzin round, sticky melon juice drippin down into my drawers; I felt so damned stupid. I climbed into the car and drove us out to Kern County Park as fast as I could. Whenever we got there I kicked the livin shit out of Clyde Mays.

After we'd been there a hour or so, I barfed up all the beer I'd drunk. What a wasted day. Then a damned deputy he drove up just when Bobby Joe Hurd was pukin, and caught us with what was left of the beer we'd stole. We all got sent to juvie that time.

BSF

Next summer I was fishin in a canal out by Greenfield
with a pole I'd swiped from Thriftys. Geneie Hicks was with
me; we wasn't catchin nothin. There was one big colored
lady up the bank from us, but she wasn't doin too good
either.

Anyways, up drove this beat-lookin station wagon with
old, cracked wood peelin off the sides. And guess who got
out: the lady that busted the watermelon on me, and Nola
Sue the harelip. They had these real long poles tied to one
side of the wagon, and they commenced loosenin em. I pulled
my cowboy hat down over my eyes and just set there a-hopin
they wouldn't see me.

They finally got their poles untied, and come walkin
up the bank. The mean lady never even noticed me, but
damned if that harelip gal didn't, her eyes lockin in on me
whenever she passed, then glancin back all the time after
they got their rigs in the water up the canal. Geneie Hicks
seen her and said: "Damn but that's a ugly girl yonder."

"You ain't shittin," I answered, not lookin up.

"Does she know you from somewheres? She's surely
lookin you over."

"Let's get out of here," I told him. "We can drive up
Kern Canyon and catch us some trout."

"Sounds good," said Geneie, so we packed up our gear
and toted it back to my Chevy. Parked right next to me was
the big old Caddy that the colored lady drove. It was un-
locked, so I swiped some cigarettes and two of them wire
seat cooler things and a blanket from it; the glove compart-
ment and the trunk was locked, though. Just as I threw the
stuff from the Caddy into my car, I heard a voice say: "I
sneen nya."

I turned around and, ugly as a sinner's soul, there Nola
Sue stood. "Mind yer own bee's wax," I snapped at her.

"I won' tnell on nya."

"Thanks a lot," I said real sarcastic, then climbed into
my Chevy and got the hell away from there. She give me
the creeps, and I didn't want her old lady seein me either.

We drove out Nile Street, through the last of the
orange groves and the open hills then into the canyon. Up
by Richbar, we seen a couple cop cars and a ambulance and

a fire truck. We stopped and this here fat lady she run right up to my window and stuck her head in: "A Mexcan drownded," she hollered, "right in the river, and skindivers is lookin for im." The lady's eyes was all wide, and she kindly panted. Before I could answer her, another car pulled behind us, and she run back to it.

I parked the car and me and Geneie we walked over to where a crowd of folks was watchin them skin divers. Off to one side of us two Mexcans set on a log with their arms around this here Mexcan girl. None of em was cryin.

"It don't look half-bad," I heard one old boy say to his wife. "Hell, I could swim it easy." I poked Geneie in the ribs and whispered: "L.A." He laughed. Them bastards from down south thought they could do anything, but me, I knew about the river; pullin along lookin smooth and easy, it had one hell of a suck; I liked to got drownded there my-ownself back when I's fourteen.

Old Geneie he's real comical. He poked me back, and whispered out the corner of his mouth: "Well, hell, it looks like the Mexcans cinched the Kern River Sweepstakes for this summer. This here's about the twentieth one that drownded, and ain't but a dozen Okies done er. I sure hate losin to Mexcans. But at least we ain't last. Niggers ain't drownded but five or six, and I don't believe they's been a Chinaman or Jap or Flip done er yet." I like to split a gut tryin not to laugh out loud. Old Geneie he never even grinned: "I shore hate to lose," he said.

They had them one hell of a time findin that Mexcan's body, so me and Geneie we went back to where the cars was parked and rifled the open ones. Drowndins are pretty good, like wrecks, cause folks get excited and don't lock up whenever they park. We got all the junk we could pack into my Chevy's trunk, cameras and everthing. And we found a full pint of sloe gin in a 59 Merc. It was a real good haul. We should of took off right then, but Geneie he said he'd never seen a dead Mexcan before, so we pulled two or three long times on the sloe gin and went back to the river.

Just about the time they found that Mexcan, a lady and a man came runnin up to a sheriff from where the cars was parked and they was yellin about how someone broke into

their car. Me and Geneie just looked at each other, then
mozied back toward my Chevy and got the hell out of there
before the cops got too curious.

We buzzed up to Hobo Hot Springs, and bought us
burgers at the cafe. Afterward Geneie he went up to the
campground to look for this girl he knew, so I broke out
my pole and commenced fishin. When I got upstream I seen
a campfire on a sandbar, but didn't think nothin of it except
that it was near dark and the game warden might be out
soon lookin for guys fishin late. I'd brought what was left
of the sloe gin with me, so I reeled in and set myself on a
log under this here big tree. It was real quiet up the canyon
at night; all you heard was the river a-suckin past.

Then this voice said real soft like: "Hni."

I looked up and damned if that Nola Sue wasn't standin right in front of me in this here bikini, her body all outlined against that bonfire on the sandbar, her face hid in the dark; she'd filled out some. I started to leave, then thought better of it. "Hi," I said, "what're you doin here?"

"Ny nomma an her bnoyfriend is cnookin not nogs yonder," she nodded toward the sandbar. "I sneen ya fishin."

I'd been pullin pretty good on that sloe gin, so I didn't think too straight, my head rememberin that ugly face, my pecker just seein that good body. "Set a spell," I finally said, and she come over to me, kinda slow and shy. I reached up for her hand, then pulled her down next to me, careful not to see her face. And, as it turned out, I never even had to kiss her.

After I come out of the county road camp in '65 and got me that job cleanin burlap sacks at the Sierra Bag Company, I commenced hangin out at this honky tonk, The Sad Sack. It was a real dark place out on Edison Highway where the cocktail waitresses went topless and they had this other gal that danced behind the bar stark neked. They charged a buck for a glass of beer.

What kept me goin there was this waitress named Penny who had the pinkest nipples I ever seen and pointed, and who had a face that liked to took my breath away; her mouth looked like a red flower. She got really friendly with me, cause I bought her lots of champagne to drink. It got to where I'd come in and she'd just smile at me, and all the other guys looked half-sore. They knew I was a-takin over.

Only thing was that my wages at the bag company couldn't stand them dollar beers and champagne at two-fifty a glass. Besides, I needed to buy Penny some presents, cause she wouldn't put out less I did. So I got in touch with some of the boys, and we commenced hittin gas stations pretty reg'lar, always late at night whenever there wasn't but one old boy workin. We never hurt nobody, and damned if we didn't scoop us up some money.

Penny she loved it. I told her what I was doin, and she laughed and said she was my gun moll. I bought her a new

Dodge and moved us into a nice place over on Flower Street.
She quit out at the Sad Sack and I had to step up my service
station business, her buyin clothes and all, hittin one a week
for a long spell, driving up above Fresno and clean down to
San Diego so's the cops wouldn't know where to expect us
guys next. In the back of my head I knew Penny was a
hustler, but it wasn't my head I was listenin to. I even quit
my job at the bag company, and maybe that was what really
caused me to get caught.

I come home early one day after casin a gas station
over in Arvin and caught Penny and this Mexcan makin out
on the couch; she didn't have nothin on but her drawers,
and she was doin somethin for him she hardly ever done for
me. Jesus Christ! It was damn lucky I wasn't carryin my
pistol, cause I'd of shot both of em. Still, I beat her bloody,
and stomped that Mexcan.

I left em there on the floor and drove over to Oildale
and found some of my partners at the Highland Club. There
was this big strike of Mexcans goin on out at the grape fields
north then, and most of us guys didn't like it a-tall. I mean,
they wasn't just Mexcans, which is bad enough, but they
was Commies too. I didn't have no trouble gatherin up a
gang of boys to drive out to McFarland with me to whup us
some goddamn Mexcans. I surely wanted to work over a
few of them greasy bastards. I wanted to kill em and send
em back to where they come from.

The first couple fields we seen had too many of em,
and sheriffs too. But over by Cawelo there was a small field
with mostly Flips workin in it and maybe half-a-dozen Mexcans carryin signs on a dirt road next to a irrigation ditch.
We pulled up, two carloads of us, with some clubs we'd
picked up on the way, and we pounded piss out of em and
run em off. Them Fillipinos in the fields laughed, and some
of the guys started to go after them, but I stopped em.
"Them ain't Mexcans," I said, "they're on our side." Then
this one Flip he come up to me and said there was another
bunch of greasers down the dirt road a piece. "You kill kill,"
he said, and I liked to laughed at how funny he talked. Still,
I wasn't through with goddamn Mexcans – the crooked,
greasy bastards—not by a long shot. I needed to whup me a

few more. I *needed* to, cause Penny and that spic kept flashin into my head.

Maybe some of them guys we'd beat up earlier had warned em, but the Mexcans at the next field was waitin for us. They fought like white men, and one guy, just when I's fixin to wallop him, he spun around and hit me across the bridge of my nose with a board. That's all I recollect. When I come to, I's in a hospital room. I could just barely see; my eyes nad gone all fuzzy on me. They knocked me out and done a operation, but when they finally took the bandages off, I couldn't see no better; in fact, I believe it's worse. And it got worser.

If that ain't bad enough, Penny pressed charges for assault and rape (ain't *that* a kick in the ass!); that Mexcan was hurt bad and they got me for somethin called mayhem; one of my boys told about the gas stations; the only thing they didn't charge me with was whuppin them strikers, even the cops couldn't fault me there. The public defender told me I could get life for all the stuff they had on me what with my record and all. Then he said maybe a judge would go easy since I was *blind*.

When I heard that word I wanted to bawl. Blind! That meant I wasn't goin to get no better, and the goddamn doc never even told me. Blind, and goin to jail over that damned woman and her Mexcan. That night I tried to hang myself, but I couldn't even do that right.

The public defender knew what he's talkin about. I only got 5-to-20 years at Vacaville because I was blinded. And somethin funny happened after the judge passed sentence and the court adjourned. I heard the defender say "Alright," to someone, then this small hand touched my arm: "NI'm sorry," said a voice and I knew right then who it was. Ugly gals is hard to forget.

"I don't need nobody's fuckin sympathy," I kindly spit at her, jerkin my arm away. I tried to walk away but bumped into the goddamn table.

"Cnan nI wrnite nya?"

"Leave me the hell alone," I said, then, damnit, I busted out cryin. "Dead people don't need no letters," I sobbed.
"NI'll wrnite," she said, touchin my arm. "Nyou ain' dead."

Nola Sue did write, by God, and a couple months at Vacaville surely taught me to welcome anything I got. My folks was both dead by then, and I never had no mail cept from her. After a while, she asked in a letter if she could come up and visit me. That was hard, cause there she was just a-sendin me letters and stuff, and willin to drive clean up to Vacaville but, to tell the truth, I just didn't want none of the guys up there to see me with a harelip, so I wrote her no.

Then she sent me this here tape recorder so I could send her letters without having to dictate to some other guy, and that really helped. She sent me lots of presents—Christmas, birthday, and just of the hell of it too—so I made her a leather wallet and key case, and had this other ol boy tool it all fancy. Then she wrote and asked again if she could come up; she had vacation, and she'd surely like to visit me.

I couldn't tell her no again, good as she'd been to me. So up she come, me really dreadin the whole thing. When I heard her talkin all funny, I just wanted to crawl away, but damned if I didn't forget all about the way she sounded once she was tellin all about how things was at home. And it felt mighty nice to have a woman's hand reach over and squeeze mine. It felt damned good.

I was all mixed up between being happy and sad whenever I headed back to my job at the hospital laundry. I enjoyed havin Nola Sue to talk to, but it made me feel sadder bein inside. Then I heard this one old boy kindly whistle through his teeth while I was passin, and he said to whoever was next to him: "I just seen the ugliest woman in the world. Gaw-awd damn but she was enough to gag a maggot." The other guy laughed.

"Shut your fuckin trap!" I hollered at em.

They didn't say nothin for a second, then the guy doin all the talkin he said, "What's wrong with you, pard, you're the lucky one. You didn't have to see her."

I started swingin but only messed my hands up.

I spent nearly three years inside that time, and I determined that I'd never go inside again. I just wasn't worth it.

On the day they let me go, Nola Sue was there to pick me
up. We never discussed it or nothin, but I just naturally
moved in with her whenever we got back to Oildale.

She'd helped me find a job sandin paddles at this here
new canoe factory out on North Chester, and I went right
to work when I got home. The job wasn't that much, but
between the both of us—Nola Sue worked as a beauty oper-
ator—we ate regular and even snuck in a little in savins.
Three nights a week Nola Sue drove me to school so's I
could finish my high school diploma. She helped me avoid
the boys, and she seen to it I never missed no meetins with
my parole officer either.

One afternoon I stopped after work with some fellers
from the factory for a beer. I no sooner'n set, and I heard
this familiar voice call out: "Damn if that ain't a squirrely-
lookin Okie sittin yonder!" It was that crazy Clyde Mays,
and even if the parole officer wouldn't like it, he surely
sounded good to me. "Come over here you skinny fart," I
hollered, and directly he was sittin next to me a-pumpin my
hand. "You old sack a shit," he said, "damned if you don't
look fat and sassy."

Well, we had lots of old times to talk about, and he
filled me in on where everone was now. We had us a few
more beers than I'd planned and I stayed later. Finally, I
said to him, "Wait a minute, Clyde. I got to call home so my
ol lady don't get too worried."

"What?" he asked. "You pussy-whipped by a harelip
gal? Shit, I can almost see screwin her and lettin her donate
a little money, but I sure as hell didn't think you'd be
pussy-whipped."

That pissed me. "I ain't pussy whipped!"

"You act like you really give a shit for that ugly harelip
gal," he laughed, just eggin me on.

"Talk sense!" I snapped. "Tail's tail, and blind guys
don't get much choice."

"I 'precciate that," Clyde went on, "but don't let no
woman get aholt to you, bo, or you'll damn sure take a
pussy-whippin."

"Well I don't give a shit for her, so shut up about it!"
He did, and we talked a while longer, but the fun was gone.

Whenever I got home that night, Nola Sue asked if I'd eat and when I said I hadn't she went into the kitchen. Me, I set in the livin room and turned on the radio so I could listen to some good country music. I didn't feel too hot and it wasn't just the beer I'd drunk. Directly, she come in and put a T.V. tray in front of me and told me where things was on it. I didn't like the sound of how she talked, all n-sounds, so I just said "Shut up and leave me be!"

She did, takin herself back into the kitchen, then I heard her cryin, snortin in that funny way harelips do. Old Stoney Edwards come on the radio and went to singin about how his woman was his rock. Well, I set there awhile, that beer a-workin in me, and I heard Nola Sue had quit cryin in the kitchen. Somethin in me wanted to apologize, but I couldn't be pussy whipped by no harelip, so I rared up and hollered for her to come out from the kitchen, me puffin like a ol bull I's gettin myself so worked up.

Soon as I heard her shuffle kinda close I raged at her: "I don't need no goddam harelip!" But I no sooner'n got the words out than somethin wet and hot salted my cheeks. "I don't need no goddam harelip," I said again, my lower lip commencin to shiver so bad I couldn't hardly talk.

I waited for her to bawl some, but she never, and my own face just wouldn't get under control. She never said nothin, and I could only hear my own breath snortin, makin me wonder in my darkness if the whole thing wasn't just a beer dream, and maybe I's alone, stuck in a cell somewheres, or maybe just inside myself. Then I felt her hand, cool and real, on my face. I wanted to slap it away, but I couldn't move, so I blubbered one more time: "I don't need no goddam harelip."

She had both hands on my face then, cradlin it, and she answered: "No, but nyou need a woman."

And she was right.

Silver Bullet

You boys don't recollect ol Slim Barney Barnes, I reckon, but he's one hell of a worker in his day. Only thing was he rubbed folks the wrong way. He's what you'd call your basic smart ass. Wasn't nothin he didn't think he knowed. Claimed he could've went to college on a scholarship but he never wanted to. I guess he wanted to be a bindle stiff instead.

Barney he read all these pamphlets he got from some-wheres and he'd tell you in a minute about niggers and Mex-icans how they was pawns of International Jewry, and how they was bent on takin things over from "True Americans," meanin him and you, mostly him. He kept quotin some old boy named Gerald L. K. Smith that knew all the true facts about the Jews, like how old Roosevelt hisself was one, and the Pope in Rome was in on it. And the Reds. Wasn't nothin Slim Barney couldn't tell you bout how to run the world.

So whenever he come to work out to Mettler Station where I's buckin hay, I figured he'd chew my ear off with true facts. Bigger'n hell, that very first night I's settin in Peaches & Jim's, this cafe next to the highway, sippin a brew whenever old Slim Barney slipped onto the stool next to me. He rushed through his howdys, then got right to the point: "What kind of gun you carry?"

"Gun?" I liked to laughed right then cause Barney's so damn serious.

"Yeah, gun. You keep a gun handy don't ya?"

"Cain't say as I do."

"No gun!" His wirey old neck stretched out some. "What're ya gonna do when *they* come?"

"They?" says I, just shy of a grin, fightin not to laugh.
"Who?"

"WHO!" It looked like his eyes was gonna pop out;
his chicken neck liked to stretched another foot. "The niggers! The niggers, that's who!"

I told him I never figured too many niggers was hot
for my bedroll in the bunkhouse and ten-hour-a-day buckin
hay, but they was welcome. Besides there was half-a-dozen
colored guys working around that big old farm anyways.

"See there!" he busted out. "Them's spies! They wanta
screw all the white gals!"

"No more'n I do," I laughed.

He jumped up. "All right!" he shouted. "All right! See
if I care whenever the Pope of Rome makes you kiss his
ring!"

"Kiss my ass," I told him, and he took off.

We was workin for a really big outfit then, one of them
corporate farms that's got cattle and sheep and hay and
grapes and you name it spread all over hell. One guy on
my crew he'd worked for the same outfit clean over in New
Mexico where they had livestock and grew short staple.
Our bunkhouse, the one closest to Mettler Station, was in
the remains of a old ranch house, and there was still a wind-
mill, tank, and barn, and right next to the house, a old family
graveyard with faded wooden markers. The company had
built a huge aluminum barn—bigger than all the other build-
ings put together—and there was trucks and tractors and
thousands of sacks of chemicals in there, and a office with
typewriters and everything.

But us hands, we bunked in that old ranch house, and
most of us liked it because it was like old times. Even old
Slim Barney seemed to settle in purty good, though he kinda
scooted his bunk a little off to itself, and he brought in this
wooden grape crate and lined up all his pamphlets and
booklets and tracts so's he could get to em in a hurry if
some old boy was to doubt the true facts.

A week or so after I'd told him to kiss off, Slim come
a-slidin up to my bunk with a funny look on his face. "See
that greaser yonder?" he nodded. I told him yeah. "Well I
hear he claims he usta be a cowboy. Ain't that somethin, a

goddamn Mesican. Old Johnny Mack Brown'd make tacos out of him."

"He did," I said.

"Made tacos out of him?"

I give Slim a hard look. "Naw. That old man — his name's Jesus Garcia—he used to ride up at the Tejon Ranch."

"*The* Tejon Ranch! Hell!" He squatted right on the floor. "Scrawny old bugger like him workin a real ranch. Yer shittin me."

I don't like nobody to call me a liar, even if its as sorry a specimen as Slim Barney, so I called Jesus over. Now Jesus he's a good old boy, friendly and honest as a dollar bill. Talk your damn nuts off, though. He shuffled over and plopped on the bunk next to me (Barney not likin that a-tall). "Jesus," I said, "this here skinny fart is Slim Barney Barnes, a guy I knowed from way back."

Jesus stuck his horny old hand out, and I seen Barney hesitate. I figured he's about to take a whippin right then, cause Jesus was still plenty handy, and Barney he fought about as good as old folks fuck. Finally, Slim Barney stuck his hand out for a quick shake, then wiped it on his jeans. Jesus never noticed.

"Barney here, he'd like to hear about the old days up on the Tejon. He's a Johnny Mack Brown fan."

"Who?" asked Jesus, and this time Barney give me a hard look.

"It don't matter," I said. "Tell him about that time you boys found that haunted lodge."

"An the Boscos?"

"That's it," I said.

Jesus crossed his legs and rolled a cigareet. "Wal me an Sharlie Wilson we's ridin over by San Emidio, and this American guy he comes up to us all crazy, screamin, sayin come right away now, one of the Boscos — he calls em Basques or somethin—one of them Boscos is dead. He tol us where and took off, eh. So we wen over there, an there was this big casa de campo, you know, logia, an it was hid in this canyon I never even know it was there until this American guy, eh," Jesus paused for a long pull at his smoke, and

BJF

Barney give me another funny look, him not being used to the long-winded stories these old vaqueros can tell.

   "So wen me an Sharlie got to this logia, an we wen inside it was all empty cept for a dead Bosco under some cheepskins, so we took him out an buried him an said bendícion and seen it was gettin dark so we rolled our beds out under a big ol tree nex to that logia, eh," he nodded, but his voice, like always, never had no tone, just buzzed on sorta like radio static. "An when I was bout sleepin, I heard this funny soun like shains rattlin, so I says 'Sharlie, you hear that?' 'Hal, yeah,' Sharlie says. An for a minute we was quiet an we never heard nothin more, then the shains rattled again, an I could tell it was comin from that logia, so me and Sharlie lit torshes and we wen over there and wen inside and dint see nothin. We looked and looked and dint see nothin at all. So we wen back to our beds, but them shains kept rattlin so we never got much sleep, and I kept sayin my rosario, eh."

Barney, he was gettin impatient, and he kept lookin around like he had some place to go. Soon as Jesus paused to puff his cigareet, Old Slim he kinda stood and stretched and said: "I believe I'll mosey over to Peaches & Jim's for coffee." I reached over and, real casual, grabbed his skinny arm and squeezed hard enough to turn his hand blue, sayin "Why don't you set a spell longer and let Jesus here finish his story." Slim set.

"Nex morning me and Sharlie we wen into that logia again and seen big prints burned right into the ceilin, like a two-legged cheep been walkin up there on hot feet, and I knew it was el Diablo so we rode away fast as we could an wen over to San Emidio. After we finish our work there, me and Sharlie wen back to the main ranch an we brought some Boscos to get their frien's body where we buried him. When we got there the logia was gone like it wasn't never there, but we foun that body an lef an I never wen back there no more, eh."

Jesus uncrossed his legs and dropped the teensiest butt you ever seen on the floor; I never could figure how a man could hold a cigareet when there wasn't nothin but hot and ashes, but that vaquero could. "I gotta go now," he smiled, and he shuffled back to his bunk and plopped down and went right to sleep.

Barney waited till the old man was gone, then he spit: "Never believe nothin a Mesican says. They're taught to lie from birth; I read about in this book I got."

"What'd you think a that story?"

"Superstition, devil worship, it's all part of the International Communist Anti-Christ Conspiracy, by God! Ain't nobody but a Mesican or a nigger'd take devils and ghosts and shit like that serious. White folks know better, that's why they're white."

"Is that right?"

"Damn rights!" he barked, then he swaggered off to Peaches & Jim's.

Our work lasted into the fall and then the winter, that

outfit we's workin for had so many different things goin that
a man could stay busy. The tule fog it come in early that
year and thick, thicker'n you can believe, and if you ain't
never been in tule fog, boys, you ain't been in fog. I mean
you reach up to pick your nose and get your eye by mistake
the fog's so thick. It's tough stuff to work in, and even
tougher after work, cause you cain't do nothin or go nowheres. And colder'n a banker's heart.

We'd set around the bunkhouse tryin to play checkers
or just shoot the shit, and ol Slim Barney'd be makin a
bunghole outa hisself, tryin to tell everone bout everthing,
looking for arguments so's he could go run to his box and
grab a booklet and drop a few true facts on whoever it was.
There was one other funny thing about ol Slim: he always
wore this old fashioned nightshirt to bed, which gave the
boys a laugh, since most of em just slept in their drawers
and to hell with it.

Ever since the fog had got so bad, it no sooner'n got
dark than most of the older Mexican fellers they commenced crawlin into bed early and pullin the covers over
their heads. I asked ol Jesus about it one night just when
he's fixin to turn in, and he crossed them legs of his. "Wal,"
he said, "when the bruma de tule comes, it brings with it
many espectros..."

I stopped him. "What's them?"

"You know, *espectros*. Fantasmas." I didn't know that
one either, so he called to this other old Mexican man across
the room, and that feller called back "Ghosts." Jesus turned
to me. "Ghosts," he said.

"Ghosts?"

"Many come in bruma de tule, an they look for new
bodies they can get an...ah...escape from the bruma..."

"Bullshit!" It was Slim Barney. "I never heard nothin
like that before."

I started to tell Barney to mind his own gaddamn business, but ol Jesus he never even sounded pissed when he
went on.

"The ghosts are there, eh," he said, and he turned in.

The worst thing was that Slim come over and set on
my bunk then and got goin on how Roosevelt had started

World War Two by makin our navy be settin ducks for ol
Hirohito, and how the Nips're really Mexican race mon-
grelizers, and how we had to protect the purity of the white
race from Eye-talians like the Pope of Rome, and how it
was the Jews gettin rich for all the work we done, and don't
let ol Kovakovich tell you he's a Armenian, he's really a
Rooshian spy.

"Good night," I said.

Must of been about midnight whenever the wind got
started, and that's when the old gate on the graveyard fence
started squeekin and bangin. "What the hell's that?" I heard
ol Slim Barney sing out.

"Sounds like the gate," I answered.

"Well somebody latch the sombitch." Nobody moved,
so he called to the young guy that slept next to the door.
"Manuel, go latch that goddam gate, will ya."

"Hal no!" Manuel called back, his voice soundin
strange.

"You, Joaquin, cain't you get er?" Joaquin never even
answered. "What the hell's wrong with everone?" asked
Slim Barney.

Jesus's voice come out of the dark: "Espectros de la
bruma!"

"Spectators and brooms my ass!" shouts Slim, who's
caught on by now and acts like he's enjoyin it. "Growed men
afraid of ghosts! Ain't this somethin. Reckon the boogie
man's fixin to get ya?"

"Barney," I told him, "fix it yourself and shut up."

"By God, I will! I damn sure will! Ain't no make-believe
boogie man ghosts scares a white man, by God!" He rolled
out of his fart sack and lit the lamp, standing there in that
long white nightshirt, then he commenced rummagin in his
duffle bag and come up with a worn-lookin pistol.

I laughed. "I thought there wasn't nothin out there,"
I said.

"I ain't afraid of no ghosts," he said, "but maybe there's
a robber or somethin, by God."

"It won't do no good, eh," come this voice from a teeny
crack between the blankets on Jesus's bed. "Only silver bullets stop espectros, an only bullets of pure silver cause if

you make a bullet an there's other metal in, then you gon die cause it only hurts espectro an then it goes loco and sucks everyone's souls an..."

"By God, I'm the only one's man enough to do er, so I'll do er my way!" Slim pulled on his boots and, pistol in one hand, out he went, lookin like a ghost hisself in that long white nightshirt. Wasn't but a minute and he's back in, this highfallutin grin on his face. "Ghosts, huh, you chicken-shits. Ain't nothing wrong out there but the hasp needs fixin! He he he!" He went to the tool box and pulled out a hammer and a couple of nails, laughin all the time, and out he went again, leavin his pistol on his bed.

I crawled out of bed and walked over to the window to watch him, but I couldn't hardly pick him out. That fog it was still there, but the wind was gustin so that it looked like big white tumbleweeds rollin by. Then I seen old Barney all knelt down next to the graveyard gate drivin a nail into that hasp. He knelt there for a minute, then he stood up and the wind gusted pretty bad, rattlin the windows, and I seen him shiver, then he started back to the bunkhouse.

He stopped real sudden just a step from the gate and he had the damndest look on his face. I seen him kinda lean forward a might, ease up, then lean forward again, his face gettin tighter and tighter ever second, his neck startin to stretch. Then I seen one more thing: that fool had went and nailed the tail of his nightshirt into the hasp, and it was caught there, or *he* was, but Slim Barney never saw what had him because he never turned around. I guess all that courage just headed for parts unknown whenever he felt somethin tuggin at him from the graveyard. He couldn't get the guts up to turn around.

His face was swole like a bloated hog's when he finally screamed, and his feet commenced spinin quick as a truck's tires in compound low; his arms was pumpin and rocks was flyin behind him, his boots moving fast but goin nowheres so it seemed like sparks was shootin from em. I knowed somethin had to give quick and it did: Slim's nightshirt parted and it looked like he's shot from a gun, faster'n a silver bullet and neked as a jaybird cept for his boots and that hammer, he flew off toward Peaches & Jim's.

After them deputies brought Barney back from where they found him runnin down the highway, most of the boys had one hell of a laugh, but not ol Jesus Garcia. "Dint I tol you, eh?" he asked. Slim Barney never answered.